A Chorus of Swans

Gabriel Stone

First published 2015 in Great Britain
by The Falston Gazette Press
www.falstongazette.co.uk
Copyright © Gabriel Stone

10 9 8 7 6 5 4 3 2 1

The right of Gabriel Stone to be identified as the Author of this work has
been asserted by him in accordance with the Copyrights, Designs and
Patents Act 1988.

ISBN 978-0-9930624-4-5

With thanks to Laura
'Aided by Lolly'

Contents

Throwing Stones

John Phillip Bachmann. Born July 10th 2165. Died 19th October 2211. Possibly the 20th, if he breathes shallow.

'Nice landing Tess.' Even if she could hear me, my sarcasm would have been a waste of precious breath. It's only been a day since her vocal interface went down and I can't get out of the habit of talking to her. Her primary supercooler was shot too; that slowed her down, made her think about things a while, but boy could she think. I phased out for a spell at the pre-launch briefing - I can't even remember why she's called T.E.S.S, though I'm almost sure the 'ss' part stands for 'synaptic subsystems' - but there was something else about revolutionary problem solving algorithms based on probability analysis and chaos mathematics.

'Chaos is right.' I try shifting in the flight seat and wince. It's not just the ship that's broken; I won myself a couple of cracked ribs and my left shoulder isn't attached to the rest of me like it's supposed to be. Could

9

have been worse though. My EVA suit cushioned most of the impacts after my harness snapped and I bounced around the flight deck like some cockamamie beach ball. In a higher grav environment all they'd have found of me would have been a suit full of mush.

Have to say, I hate EVA suits. They're bulky and inflexible, and oppressive enough to turn anybody into a claustrophobe. And they stink. The air and waste recycling systems work fine for a couple of hours, but stay in a suit for much longer than that and you'll be wearing a sewer. I've been in EVA-RS3 for twenty-two of the last twenty-six hours, and the acrid stench is so bad it's stinging my eyes and I'm fighting not to gag after every breath.

Twenty-six hours? Is that all it's been since the accident, if you can call going stir-crazy and trying to bug out in a shuttle without opening the bay doors an accident? Tess hadn't seen that one coming. Seems that the most unpredictable and chaotic thing in the universe is people, and for all her smarts Tess had no way of knowing what was going on in Comms Technician Morrison's head. Morrison had lost it and died taking the shortest shuttle flight in history; the rest of the crew had followed him in stages, each playing out their final scene on the flight deck monitors: Stanislav and McCray were incinerated when the explosion ripped through the mess; Jefferson, Bailey and Crean made an unscheduled trip off-ship when the main power conduit blew and tore a hole in the starboard hull plating; Peterson, Turner, Chang and Poe drowned in their stasis tubes when the cryo deck shut down.

That left Gross and Lester.

Gross and Lester were my friends, and you can't say that about many of the slugs you ship out with.

Gross and Lester were my friends, and right now I can't remember what either of them looked like.

Gross and Lester were my friends, and I'm not exactly sure how they died. I do know they'd still been alive when the camera in the main connecting corridor went dark. There's a chance they suffocated when The Excalibur's air had finally bled-out; more likely the massive radiation leak from the FTL core got them first. Either way, the banging on the flight deck hatch stopped after about an hour. I'd thought about opening that hatch, but that would have let clean air out and dirty air in. There were three EVA suits in the flight deck storage lockers, but only one of them had a full tank and I didn't relish the prospect of drawing straws to see who got to breathe longest. No doubt you're going to judge me for that call, but I'm way past caring about how history is going to view my actions, and frankly I really don't think anybody is going to give a shit about my morally dubious self-preservation back on Earth. Not when I'm dragging nearly five million tons of part-refined mineral ores along with me. That much candy can sweeten the smell of a whole lot of stink, assuming there's anybody left there to give a shit about anything at all, of course. Things were already pretty bad when I left, and without the stuff I'm hauling to replenish the atmo cleaners the only option would be enforced relocation to the colonies to try and get the population down. Great plan; now that we've had some practice screwing a planet up, I'm sure we'll do it much faster and more efficiently on Mars and Europa. I'd take my chances on a dying Earth rather than live on one of those low-grav gaspers.

According to The Excalibur's fault location systems things weren't as bad as I'd first thought. Most of Tess' interface systems were offline, so I had to resort to the keyboard to communicate with her. In turn, she had no way of responding to me other than by doing what I asked, but at least her primary processors seemed to be intact. Better still, most of the secondary systems were still working, so Tess could still control, and most importantly navigate, the crippled ship. As for the damage to The Excalibur, the pressure doors had sealed off the hull breach and the fires in the mess and storage bays had been snuffed when the air ran out. The problem was power. Electrical failures were happening all over the ship, and unless I found a way to deal with them The Excalibur would die slowly, one system at a time. With power restored the cryo tanks would come back online, the electromagnetic shielding around the FTL core would contain the radiation leak and reactivate the drive pre-heaters, the air scrubbers and emergency re-breather system would kick-in, and the decontamination protocols would start automatically. Not only would that be enough to keep me alive, it would be enough to get me home. An hour earlier I would have called that a miracle; an hour later I needed another one.

The damaged power conduit was beyond the pressure doors in a section of the ship now open to space, so repair wasn't an option. A damn fine engineer might be able to route main power via the secondary couplings though, so it's a good thing that the reason I was riding this tram in the first place was because I was a damn fine engineer. Then came the real kicker. Secondary power coupling R14-A, the one right here under the main flight console, wasn't up to the job. I could rig a replacement with a higher rating, but to do that I'd need an ounce or so of pure rhodium. Enough for a part roughly the size and shape of a toothpick.

I had to laugh; seemed like the thing to do. Dead for the lack of an ounce of rhodium on a ship with a hundred tons of the stuff in the aft cargo bays, impossible to get to and useless now that it had been irradiated. 'Hey Tess, did they ever teach you about irony?'

I stopped laughing.

Tess!

Tess was the answer; I had just been asking the wrong question. I'd been making her nibble on details when she should have been chewing on the big picture. That I could fix.

I had to gasp for breath as I moved to the keyboard. The air on the flight deck had tasted wrong for a while; now it felt like my lungs were rejecting it. Tunnel vision made typing hard. Keys too small. Keep it simple. Three words. Just three words.

I typed 'GET ME HOME'. Simple. Direct. Short.

Then everything went dark.

I woke up to the worst headache of my life, but even through the pain I could tell that things had changed whilst I'd been away. For starters, I could breathe without feeling like I was going to puke. Secondly, The Excalibur's engines were running. Not the FTL drive, just the main thrusters; I could feel their vibration through the deck. It didn't take much investigation to figure what had happened. I could breathe because when I'd blacked out, Tess had followed emergency protocols and dumped the reserves of uncontaminated air onto the flight deck. Better still, the engines were lit because The Excalibur had somewhere to be. According to the nav display, we were en route to asteroid BR-4552. At seventeen kilometres on the longest edge it was a big sucker, but there was no significant info on file because it hadn't been fully surveyed yet. This far out they rarely took a close look at these boulders, even the really big ones, unless their paths took them into Earth's solar system, and BR-4552 didn't even get close. Good thing too; this piece of rock had 'extinction event' written right through it.

So why were we going there?

I was reaching for the keyboard when a footnote flashed up on the nav readout. It said 'Mining Potential'.

That was it; Tess must have detected rhodium on BR-4225. My guess was she was planning to land on the asteroid, use the drones to extract and process the ore, and then get the pure metal to me through the flight deck's emergency air lock. It was desperate, but if none of the important systems failed before we got there then it might work.

Damn she was smart.

Journey time would be twenty-three hours. The air on the flight deck would last one hour at best. The EVA suit with the full tank and the partial tanks from the other suits would give me another twenty-six hours, give or take, even with the recycling systems going flat-out. That would give Tess and me no more than four hours to get the repairs to the console done and the primary systems back online.

It was going to be close.

I was connecting the last near-empty tank to my suit when the engines kicked in hard. We were five minutes from touchdown and I'd been expecting the familiar tremble of the landing struts extending. Instead I got an earthquake as the thrusters switched to full burn, turning final approach into a crash-dive. I wasted a few lungfulls of precious air screaming at Tess to shut off the engines. Too late I remembered that she couldn't hear me, and there was no hope of typing fast with the EVA suit's chunky plastic fingers. All I could do was strap in and wait for the impact.

Thirty seconds before that impact came, Tess jettisoned the flight deck to send it careening over the surface of BR-4552 whilst the rest of The Excalibur slammed into the asteroid, the silent devastation made all the more surreal by the low gravity. The flight deck pod jolted to a halt as the emergency landing harpoon deployed and kept me anchored to this nothing lump of rock. Remotely firing the harpoon was to be Tess' last act before a section of hull plating went clean through her brain pan.

I reach for the keyboard but the pain in my side pulls me up short. There's no point anyway; Tess is dead.

In ninety-seven minutes, I will be too. I'm planning to spend most of that time laughing.

Because I've worked it out.

Tess never intended to mine rhodium on this asteroid. She'd probably known all along that there was none here to mine. It made no sense until it sunk in to my thick skull that the crash was no accident or dumb miscalculation.

It was a nudge.

Not much of one, given the size of BR-4552, but enough to cause a miniscule change in the asteroid's course and rotation. Doubtless Tess had even allowed for the mass of The Excalibur's debris and payload when she'd calculated the new trajectory. Who knows, she might even have included my slowly rotting corpse in that calculation.

I asked her to get me home, and that's exactly what she's done, the only way she could think of.

Damn she was smart.

John Phillip Bachmann. Born July 10th 2165. Died 19th October 2211. Returned home March 16th 3146. Impact coordinates N.41.28.46 E.135.0.0. Sea of Japan.

A Bird in the Hand

Sure, why not? Stand me a shot and I'll tell you about it. Make it a double and you can have the whole damn story. You'll laugh till you pop a lung. The good shit too? Well thanks. You can be my best pal till I sober up. So park yourself and I'll tell you about my arm and the last glassbird. The glassbird? You not heard of it? Guess it was a few years back, and now you mention it you hardly look old enough to be buying booze. Not that anybody in this dump would care even if you weren't. Well if you don't know about glassbirds then I suppose I'd best start right at the beginning. Story will take a shitload longer to tell that way, so I might be needing a refill before the end.

Reckon it was around 2317 when the first survey team landed on 2208-UBL414. They had to send a team in because probes could see jack through the atmosphere, and no transmissions could get through it either. Had to do with magnetic fields, ionisation layers, static discharge, some technical shit like that. Don't know the science, just know that the only way to find out what was on the surface was to go down there and take a look-see, and the only way to tell anybody what you'd look-seen was to fire relay buoys up out the atmosphere. Central hates planets with shitty comms; they don't feel in control if you don't check in every five minutes. The comms on 2208-UBL414 were the shittiest.

UBL414. As far as I know they still ain't given that goddamn planet a real name, but when the first pictures were beamed back people took to calling it New Eden because they thought it looked pretty. Morons. Okay, I guess it did look kinda impressive if you were into trees and flowers and shit, and it was a hellavalot better than most of the other spinning piles of garbage they'd found with halfway decent gas to breathe, but then that was the problem, see? The place got to be big news. People wanted to know everything about everything about UBL414. Joe Ordinary took to reading the discovery journals instead of using them as toilet paper. First thing they worked out was the place was too far away to be any good for stripping. No mining company was going to turn a profit hauling stuff from that far out, and those eco nuts would have made one hellava noise if anybody had tried it anyway. Next thing they worked out was that there was a bundle of cash to be made from 414. Colonization was all it was good for and there were plenty who wanted to go there, and when a shitload of people want the same thing but there ain't enough of it to go round then the price goes up real quick. The place was beautiful they reckoned, and that was enough, just like with people; inside they might be nothing but crap, but if the crap comes in a snazzy bag, who cares about the smell? Take Melinda over there. Yes, that's her, the blonde with the legs. Now she can't count to sixteen without taking both boots off, and if you dropped dead in here ol' Melinda there would empty your pockets before you hit the floor, but there's not a fella in this joint who hasn't been down on his knees begging her to be his girl, and that includes yours truly. Not that bums like us have much chance with the likes of that one. The road between that girl's legs got a tollbooth on it, and even those that can afford to ride had best be doing it in a stretch limo or they ain't going to be keeping her satisfied. So long as you've got cash she don't care if you can't talk the talk, but when you walk the walk she wants to see some pendulum action going on. But hell, when you're down there on your knees begging, with your face up so close to....what? Oh yeah, the glassbird. Damn, that Melinda has a way of making a man's mind go a wandering, if you know what I mean. All I'm saying is that when something looks that fine you don't waste braintime thinking about it, you just want it bad. That's how it was with 414. Soon as people saw those first pictures they wanted it bad. Central tried to stop it, but some of the land allocation agencies were selling plots on that rock before they had any legal say-so. Whole planet was parcelled up and sold off before the survey team had taken a step out the lander. Big development companies queued up for their meal tickets, and for a while there it looked like everybody was going to get their fill. Everybody who could afford to, anyhow. Then the whole crock of beans blew up in their faces when the survey team found the glassbirds. See there are all sorts of rules and red tape when a planet has indigenous animal life. Nobody gives a damn about flowers or trees. Planets with plant life were a dime a dozen even back then, but animals are a different story. A purple tree on another planet is still just a purple tree, but an animal on another planet is an *alien* see, and people just love their aliens. Higher life forms and all that bull, and until 414 the highest any other planet had come up with were those stinking leechrats on Spinnica. Ever seen one of those things? Jesus, those buggers are just plain nasty, and I ain't even going to talk about the stench. There was plenty of hoo-ha about Spinnica when they found those leechrats, but nothing like the stir that 414 got going. It was the glassbirds they found first, but there was plenty more to find. Regular zoo it was. More life in one place than anybody had ever seen. Some said there were more types of plants and animals there than on Earth back in the old days. Never been to Earth? Can't say I blame you. Got shipped back there to get my arm fixed up. Can't say I'm in any hurry to go back. Reckon that's why 414 got into people's heads like it did; reminded them of what Earth was supposed to be like. What it *was* like, before we screwed it over. Back before we sent those big 'ol refinery ships off into the deep black to find more of the shit that Earth had run out of. Some damn fool once said that those ships didn't leave with empty cargo holds, they left full of hope. Guess all that hope left no room for anything else, 'cos not a one of those ships ever came back.

It's kinda ironic that we screwed 414 over just the same as on Earth, only we did it faster. Practice makes perfect I guess. So anyways, the place had all kinds of shit living on it. Primeval they called it, which as far as I can tell just meant that there were plants and animals and nothing else. Nothing smart. Nothing we could talk to. Some said that we should leave it alone and let evolution carry on down whatever road it was already travelling. Said that us being there would mess it all up. Guess they wanted us to wait around a few million years until there was somebody there to complain about us stealing their planet. The way I see it, Central had been playing the odds with the whole indigenous life manifesto anyhow. They came up with it when most of their scientists reckoned there was none out there to be found, and they got away with pretty much ignoring it on Spinnica 'cos nobody with any real say gave a damn about leechrats and stinkworms. Problem with Spinnica was they needed bio domes. Nobody can breathe the stale fart that passes for air on that rock for more than a few minutes at a stretch, and domes means spending money. Money they ain't got. Then they find 414. Planet with an atmosphere that don't make a man puke turns up when there's land riots going on all over the place, but now they can't let people go there right away because of those 'seemed like a smart idea at the time' indigenous life rules. Real clever that, making it so's that when they get themselves a gift horse it turns round and kicks them square in the balls. That must have been tough for Central to swallow, and there's plenty there I'd like to see swallow their own balls, but it's the glassbirds that really stuck in their craw. Now I'm not one who thinks much on critters, except maybe how they'd taste swimming in gravy with sourmash and greens, but I went real soft on those glassbirds, same as everyone else did. Big as a full-grown man - double counting the tail - and real sparkly. Yeah, that's what I said, sparkly. No other word fits as snug. See glassbirds had feathers all right, and they could fly just fine when they got a mind to, but not feathers like on ordinary birds. Glassbirds' feathers were like flat crystals, same as those big silica plate semiconductors in Warlberg engine valves, real thin and light but real strong too. And transparent, so you should have been able to see right through to the skin. They'd have been ugly suckers then, all raw and plooky like new plucked chickens. Guess things might have turned out different if they *had* been sour to look at. But you couldn't see through to the skin. The way those feathers were layered made them work like prisms, only better. It was more science than I could be bothered trying to understand, but somehow those feathers could suck up light, amplify it, then spit it back out in just about every colour you can think of. Even just walking around on the ground a glassbird shone like a stained glass window that had the sun right behind it. But the real show started when it was up in the air and those crystal wings had to work for their keep. Climate was hot and wet on 414, lot of water in the air. Sometimes it felt like it was rain that wasn't moving, big ol' drops just floating there in front of your face, and when a glassbird was flying all that wet in the air made a ten metre rainbow that hung onto its tail and got pulled along behind. Survey team shot some video of a whole flock. Must have been a thousand of them flying over their camp, and when that went onto the public networks you'd have thought it was a movie of God himself. When we're done here you could go search the archives and take a look. Central kept a lot of the 414 stuff quiet, even tried to go back and clean up some of their shit before too many folks stepped in it spread the stink around, but that vid should still be there somewhere.

So Central couldn't let anybody settle on 414, but there was nothing said they couldn't sell permits to visit the place to take a look-see. Or more expensive permits to collect specimens for 'scientific study'. There were permits to be had for damn near anything. Reckon if you waved enough cash around you could get a 'paint yourself green and do your sister in the ass before taking a dump in your hat' permit, so long as you didn't want to live on 414 afterwards. Central got those permits out fast too. Took three years to get the safety and quarantine inspections done on Spinnica. On 414 they sent inspectors in with the second survey team and got the medical clearances through in less than a month. Yeah, I'm talking Earth time, don't hold with this new standard time bull. All happened so quick that a lot of smart types got to thinking that Central were trying to pull something, but I guess they weren't smart enough to figure out what that something was. Didn't need to be smart though to see that the rules that came with those expensive permits were messed up. You had to set up camp where Central said - that's not so strange, was the same sort of deal on Spinnica - but everybody who had one of the first batch of permits, and there were 5,000 of them, had to go to 414 at the same time. That *was* strange. Central made sure it happened that way by making it a rule that nobody could go there in their own ship. Only legal way on or off was on Central's own shuttles, and the only shuttles Central made available were screamers. Screamers? That's what space-jocks used to call the old low orbit cargo haulers, the ones came outta Earth when the first colonies were being set up, 'cos of the God-awful noise those ion-push engines made when you ran them in atmosphere. Those things were banned on Earth a long time back, but Central reckoned they were the only ship they had enough of to get all those people and all that gear to so many different places on 414, and all at the same time. Fair enough, nothing sneaky there, right? Me? I think it was some of the sneakiest shit ever. See I reckon the scientists at Central studied all the data from the first survey team and saw right away that the magnetic fields and ionisation layers on 414 - yeah, the ones that caused all the problems with the comms - were in real delicate equilibrium, and it wouldn't take much to tip the balance and mess it all up. A couple of hundred of them ion-push engines punching holes in different places all over the planet would probably do it just fine. They'd also figured exactly how much messing up to do so that the planet couldn't support that irritating indigenous life anymore, but you and me would still be able to live there without needing domes. Guess they'd already done loads of tests on plants and animals, bombarding them with cosmic radiation and shit like that, finding out what people and Earth plants could stand compared to the stuff already on 414, just to make sure they'd figured it right. They had. Six months after they got everybody off 414 and quarantined it they said that a lot of the plants and all of the animals there were dying. Dying because of an atmospheric shift that nobody could have seen coming. They said their scientists were trying to track down the cause, but there was no evidence that our going there was anything to do with it. Eventually they went with 'extreme climatic variance caused by an as yet unidentified solar event'. Bull. Like I said, sneakiest shit ever. My grandpa was real old Earth, and he used to say shit like 'people who live in glass houses shouldn't throw stones'. Reckon Central went to 414 with all the stones they could find and a whole sackful of catapults.

Proof? Nah, course I can't prove it. Think I'd be here in this dump talking to you if I could? But I reckon somebody smart who had the inclination to stick his nose in deep enough might find something that stank.

Sit yourself back down. Hell no, that's not the end, that's just the backstory. Before I carry on though I reckon now'd be a good time for that refill.

Thanks. Ready? Nowadays 414 is just another of those conspiracy theories that people talk about like it's important, but they really don't give a damn about when it comes down to it. Back then it was 'an issue'. To show how concerned they were, Central got to rounding up as much of the wildlife and plants as they could, moving them to zoos and museums and anywhere else that would have them. Wouldn't be surprised if a critter or two that hatched on 414 ended up as a plate of mystery meat in some cheap joint like this one. Course once Central got those animals off they died pretty quick. Some in transit, most soon after. Survival rate off-world was real shitty till they realized that all that water in the air on 414 was loaded with these microbes, and without them nothing could breathe right. Once they figured how to grow those tiny suckers they were able to move stuff off 414 and keep it alive. After a couple of years they reckoned they'd found and saved all there was to save. All 'cept those glassbirds. They tried every damn thing, but they couldn't snag one alive, and every time they blew it there was one less glassbird to try and catch. They were just too fragile see. If you got one in a net they thrashed around until they smashed themselves to pieces. If you hit one with a tranq dart they kinda exploded. Same if you hit them with a laser. Laser was just too much light for those crystal wings to deal with - they'd resonate for a second then the whole damn bird would pop like a glass balloon. They killed six just trying to photograph them with cameras with laser-ranging focus before they figured that out. Drugged food never got eaten, the birds always knew somehow, and the one they tried to gas managed to smash its head open on a tree before they could get to it. Bottom line was glassbirds got spooked real easy, and when they got spooked they usually got dead. People didn't like that. Said that if all

Central could do was kill them then they should be allowed to die off in peace. No big surprise that Central agreed. They kept a chunk of the planet under quarantine and called it a 'preserve'. Colonists got the rest. Preserve? Yeah right. Place was a goddamn killing jar. Everything in there was just busy dying, and all anybody could do was go in and pick out the bodies. That's how they got a few glassbirds into museums. They didn't smash themselves up if they died a *natural* death, if you can call what we did to them natural. The quarantine stayed on that preserve for fifteen years, and for four of them nothing looked to be alive in there. Nothing 'cept trees and ferns and the other plants that were able to live through the 'extreme climatic variance'. A few bugs too, but nobody cared much about them. They could have let people in there sooner and there wouldn't have been much noise about it, but the place was mostly swamp anyways so Central was in no big hurry to get at the land. Soon as there was bupkis left in the preserve that needed preserving they sold the whole shebang to some big company that reckoned they could make plant growth additives from the swamp water. Something to do with those microbes. Anyhow, the whys and wherefores of it don't matter 'cos it didn't happen. Before handing over the cash they sent a drone camera over the place to take a good look at what they were buying. Normally that kinda thing would be done by satellite but the comms on 414 were as shitty as ever. Central would have loved their tampering to have fixed that too, but I guess you can't have everything. When they looked at the film, there it was. Flying a hundred metres below the camera, big as life and twice as beautiful, there was a glassbird. A female they said. Didn't know how they could tell that, wasn't important anyways. Lucky that in the beginning those drone cameras were made for spying so they're real quiet like, otherwise I reckon that glassbird would have got spooked and flown itself right into the ground. People who should have known about this stuff had no clue why that glassbird was still alive. Best they could do was guess that it was some sort of mutation. A freak with some genetic defect or other that had made it able to survive in the changed atmosphere. When they'd stopped thinking about that they had two other questions to think on. What to do about this freak, and could there be another one? While they were thinking on the first question they took another look-see at that film to try and answer the second question. Even going frame by frame with as much magnification and enhancement as they could use they didn't find one pixel that might have been part of a glassbird. Didn't mean there wasn't one there, just meant they didn't have it on film. They couldn't send in drones or bots to take a look. More chance a bot might scare the one bird they knew about, and now that there were towns shooting up all over 414 it was a sure bet that sooner or later something would kill that bird, or spook it bad enough for it to kill itself. Hell, one stray firework from little Jimmy's birthday party and the glassbird is extinct all over again. After a lot of meetings and 'consultations' they decided to go into the preserve to look for other glassbirds, and if there was only one then they were going to try and catch it. Grandpa would have called that 'killing two birds with one stone'. Makes me laugh when I think about that. So they needed a team that could go into an unexplored swamp with a truckload of gear to track and catch a critter that had a habit of smashing itself to shards if it so much as heard you sneeze. They knew it was damn near impossible, and so they came to me. Why me? 'Cos back then I was a man who could get the job done. Any job, so long as there was enough cash. They needed men with certain skills and certain tools, and me and my team had both. Mercenaries? Now that's a word I've not heard in a while but yeah, you could've called us that back then. We'd had dealings with Central before when they'd needed some 'urban pacification' in the land riots, and most of us had spent some time in the swamps on Spinnica when those eco nuts tried to stop the work on the domes. Compared to Spinnica the swamp on 414 should've been like a day at the beach. Sven even reckoned he'd try and work on his tan. Real ladies man was Sven - he was packing equipment that would have kept even Melinda there happy - and a thinker too. It was his idea to use a scrambler to catch the glassbird. Before you ask, scramblers are electro-pulse mines that completely screw up transmissions in the brain. Knock you down cold. You'll sleep for a while and have a real bad headache after, but they don't do any lasting damage. Don't think they do anyway. Sort of an E.M.P. for organics. Have to be real close to the target to work, but they're small and quiet, and Sven's thinking was that it would put the glassbird down before it could hurt itself, then before it recovered we'd get to it and tranq it without needing darts. Far as we knew they couldn't kill themselves in their sleep. Nobody'd tried it before 'cos nobody else had scramblers. It was Sven designed them, and we kept them as our little secret. Shit like that gave us an edge.

Kept the team small for 414. Easy job, easy money, and a big fat bonus if we caught a glassbird alive. Bigger still if it was only split three ways. Me, Sven and Daviss. Took Daviss 'cos there was nobody better at turning any old shit into food. Once we'd been in a couple of days he'd know what there was to eat, and the more he could cook up the less we'd need to haul. Thought the job would take maybe four or five weeks. Second night in, Daviss said we could ditch the ration packs and just eat the stuff he could make from the plants. Most of it tasted like crap, but for what we were being paid we could eat crap for five weeks.

Sixteen weeks.

That's how long we were in that goddamn place before we saw that fucking bird. Sixteen weeks of eating leaves and mashed up bugs. Sixteen weeks in full camo, not risking talking to each other 'cept in whispers, not able to talk to anybody outside because of the comms problems. Sixteen weeks of taking shifts up in trees with the manual binocs. Sixteen weeks of either moving through grass sharp as knife blades or wading in stinking water, both of them up to our waists. Least there were no leeches. Humidity was starting to screw with the equipment by then and we were close to chucking in and hauling out. Then I saw it. I was strapped sixty metres up on something that might have been a tree, might have been a fern, recceing a clearing about five clicks north. Wasn't even looking for the glassbird. Thought that clearing might be open enough to get a transport in to take us out. Thing was just sitting there, picking grass outta its feathers and snapping at bugs. You know, that made me mad. Damfool way to be thinking right then, but all I had in my head was how much trouble that bird had caused us in those sixteen weeks. How much trouble it had caused *me*. Had half a mind to flip the binocs over to auto and let the laser ranging fix the problem so we could go home. Yeah, I knew what the laser would do. Central had given us a big stack of documents to read about glassbirds. Most of it looked to be dreck - mating habits and shit like that - so we'd left it back in the transport. Not enough time to read it before we set out, not important enough to drag through a swamp. Only part we read was the list of what might kill it, and that was a long list. Didn't kill it though. Wanted to, but didn't. Took a bearing and got myself down from there to tell the others. That was the best few hours we had in that place, circling round slow to where I'd seen the glassbird. For a while we were even able to talk normal 'cos we knew the thing was five clicks away and looked to have been settling down for the night, and by then we were pretty damn sure there wasn't another one around to spook. We'd found ourselves the very last glassbird. All we had to do was catch it.

First night we set up half a click away and just watched. Didn't learn much, 'cept that even a glassbird looks ugly in the dark through an image intensifier. Next day was a washout. Damn bird didn't move from that same spot all day, and out in that clearing there was no way of sneaking up and putting the scrambler anywhere close to it. Then we saw that it was building some kinda nest. It scratched out a hollow and filled it with leaves and grass and whatever was close, then it parked itself on top and just went back to snapping at bugs. Sometimes it went walking around, pulling up more grass and snipping down the plants that were too tall for its liking. Seeing it do that we figured that the glassbird hadn't found this clearing, it had made it so that it would have a place to nest where it could see anything coming at it. Me and Daviss thought that was a tough break for us, but Sven didn't reckon it that way. He said that sooner or later the bird would have to go somewhere to drink or find a bigger meal, and when it did he could run in there and hide the scrambler in the nest. Soon as the bird came back and settled on top of it he could fire it by remote. Sounded like a safe enough plan to me. Next night Sven died trying it. It was near dusk, and me and Sven were eating and Daviss was on watch. Reckon he'd taken that watch so he could skip eating the shit he was cooking up. He signalled me to come over and passed me the binocs. When I looked the bird was off the nest and running across the clearing, building speed for a lift off. Glassbirds are big suckers and getting all that meat off the ground wasn't easy. Once it was up and circling to find some height we got under the camo nets and waited till it was just a flashing speck in the binocs. That was far enough for Sven. He took a charged scrambler out the pack, armed it, and made for the nest. He was most of the way there, in the last of the long grass on the edge of the clearing, when the croc got him. I was watching through the binocs, and I thought he'd just fallen at first. Then he screamed so loud that I didn't need the directional mic in the binocs to hear it, and I saw his arm come up out the grass, his big old hunting knife in his hand. His arm went down, then it came up again without the knife. There was a noise like a squealing pig and something charged off through the grass. Then Sven dragged himself, trying to get back to us. Daviss and me went and got him and carried him back to the camo nets before the glassbird came back to the nest. Sven'd passed out by then, and I was real glad of that. His right foot and had been ripped clean off at the ankle, and from the knee down his leg had been gnawed so bad I could see mostly bone. Worked on him as fast as I could with what we had in the med kit, and I got the bleeding stopped and enough drugs into him to keep him out so as not to have to deal with the pain. But I knew right off that those wounds smelled wrong. I put a tourniquet on that leg, but the poison was already going round in him. It took another four hours for Sven to die. Can't say there's such a thing as a good death, but I know that Sven's was a real bad one. His skin turned yellow, then purple, then black. His eyes went milky white and this red foam started coming out the corners of his mouth. Then his flesh started dropping off in lumps the size of my fist, sliding off his bones like meat that's been boiled too long. Worse thing I've ever seen, and the stench alone was enough to make you puke. Guess the glassbird smelled it too 'cos when I took a look out with the intensifier the damn thing was circling right over us, and if we scared it off now we might never find it again. Meant we had to stay under the net with Sven and upchuck quiet as we could. Was nearly morning by the time the bird went back to its nest, and by then Sven was dirty laundry full of shit and bones. There was no way of moving what was left. Sounds disrespectful, but truth is the best way to move him would have been with a shovel and bucket, and that would have made too much noise. Only other option was to move us, so we covered Sven best we could and broke camp. Then I sent Daviss out. He was looking freaked. I'm not saying he was a coward or anything, but in the end he was only a cook and he'd not seen death up close like that before. *Nobody* had seen death like that before. He took everything he could carry and started back for the transport. Coming in we'd been running a systematic search pattern and taking it real slow and quiet. Going out was going to be fast and straight, and we knew where the bird was now so Daviss didn't give a shit about making noise. Reckon it would take about a week if he kept up a good pace, and soon as he got to the transport he was going to fly in and pick me up. Tried to make it easier for him to go by saying it had to be him 'cos he was the better pilot, and I'd likely plough the transport into a tree before I was half way back. It was bull and we both knew it, but it helped. I kept the scramblers and the extra camo net, all the optics, and one of the plasma flares. Daviss took the other flare in case he ran into a croc. Didn't seem likely. Reckon we'd have found another croc on the way in if there was one to find, so we guessed there wasn't. Another freak, only here so's it could make a meal of the first freak. Goddamn freak show, that's what it was. Letting Daviss take the second flare meant I only had three shots when I coulda had six, but he was so strung out by what had happened to Sven that I needed him gone, and he wouldn't go without that flare. Those plasma flares were the closest thing to a real weapon we had with us, but there was no way of knowing if it would be any use against the croc. Still, it had a trigger, and I needed a trigger. If you've got a trigger then you can hurt something, and I wanted to hurt something real bad.

Daviss left about noon. Glassbird was on its nest, not moving. There was no sign of the croc, but I kept the flare launcher pushed into my belt all day anyways. Had to move position again in the afternoon and again at dusk, just to stay upwind of Sven. As it got dark I got to thinking, and when I got to thinking I got to realising that I'd screwed up. What happened to Sven must have messed with my thinking. The way I saw it I had about a week to catch the glassbird before Daviss got back with the transport, and now I knew the croc was out there I could be more careful than Sven had been. But I was on my own now, and sooner or later I was gonna have to sleep. I was too wired on that first night and there were a few stim shots in the med kit, but stims are only good for so long. I was going to get real tired.

Saw the croc again on the second morning after Daviss left. Got a good look at it this time. It was standing out in the open, near the edge of the clearing. About seven foot long and real narrow, covered in thick grey scales, with a long snout and black eyes set shallow on the sides of its head. That much of it did look like a croc. The rest was something different. It had a pair of jackrabbit legs set halfway along its body, so I guess you'd call everything from there on back its tail. Not like a normal tail that hangs down though, this was real sturdy and held three feet off the ground. Thing looked to be all muscle. Reckon I could have walked along that tail and the critter wouldn't have tipped over. Front legs were short, shrivelled things hanging down from its shoulders. Didn't use them when it walked and don't reckon they were much good for anything else neither. Thing was a predator, could see that right off, and the only prey around were the glassbird and me. Guess I wasn't on the menu for breakfast 'cos it started moving towards the nest, making a sort of gurgling sound in the back of its throat. Glassbird had already seen it, and that damn stupid bird didn't so much as twitch. It was like it was hypnotised or something. Yeah, I'd heard that some critters can do that to their prey, but I'd never seen it. Must've hypnotised me as well 'cos I couldn't take those binocs away from my eyes, just had to keep watching. The croc was just circling the clearing, watching the bird, and the bird was just watching the croc do it. When it worked round to my side of the clearing I got a look at its other flank, and that's when I saw Sven's big bastard hunting knife. It was stuck real hard in the croc's scales, in too deep to fall out but I guess too shallow to stick into anything important.

Must have been causing it a deal of pain though. That's when I had me my idea. The croc had circled round between me and the glassbird, close to the spot where it had done for Sven, and that gave me a way of running it off for a while without spooking the bird. I reached down into the pack real slow and dug around for the scrambler remote, then without even taking it out the pack I flipped the firing switch. Like I'd hoped, the armed scrambler Sven had been carrying was still in the grass where he'd fallen. It would have lost most of its charge by now, but the croc would still feel the jolt of a good size electric shock, especially with all that water in the air to help carry what charge there was. Turned out what charge there was wasn't much, but it was enough to make that croc squeal like a pig again and hop back into the long grass and disappear. And I mean hop. Must have covered six metres in that one jump. Whatever hold it had on the glassbird went with it, and that thing was up and outta the nest right away. No time to hide so I stayed where I was and stood real still. It circled up out of the clearing and headed off in the direction it had gone before, so I grabbed me a scrambler and ran for the nest. That makes it sound easier than it was. There was half a click to cover, some of it swamp, then more of that grass that could cut through your clothes, and all the time keeping a lookout for that croc. Made it though. Pushed the scrambler into the leaves deep down in the nest and started back for the camp. Tiredness was slowing down my head and my legs, and I was up to my ass in swamp before my brain got round to telling me that I hadn't armed the scrambler. Wouldn't have remembered at all 'cept I was so frazzled I was still holding the remote. I needed another stim shot bad, but they were back in the med kit and I didn't know if I had that much time or if my legs would keep moving that far and back again, so I just turned right around and went back to the nest. I was digging around for the scrambler when I saw the glassbird. It was just a flash of colour a long ways off, but it was coming, and there I was sitting in its goddamn nest. You know, even now I ain't sure how in the hell I did it, but when the glassbird glided down into the clearing I was crouched in the long grass and the scrambler was armed. Reckon my brain had gone to sleep but adrenalin kept my body doing what it was s'posed to. For the longest time that damn bird didn't go near the nest. Just kept acting crazy, strutting around making clucking noises, kicking at the ground and rubbing its tail feathers together so hard that some of them started to chip, flicking its head round like it was looking for something it knew had to be there. Guess it was looking for me. Must've been able to tell that the place had been messed with. Tried to think of some way of getting it closer to the nest without spooking it, but the stims had worn off and my brain was fried.

The croc dropped into the clearing from nowhere. Must've jumped down from a tree or something. Hadn't figured it for a tree climber, and for a big critter it landed real soft. So soft that the glassbird didn't hear. Came down about fifty metres from the nest and right away it started moving towards that dumb-ass bird, real slow and deliberate. Things were real fucked up now.

Glassbird was too far away from the nest for the scrambler, and using a plasma flare on the croc was sure to pop the bird I was s'posed to be saving. It was like watching a shuttle wreck in slow motion, where you know everybody is going to die and there's not a damn thing you can do to stop it. That glassbird was s'posed to be my meal ticket, now it was just gonna be a meal. It had other ideas though. Croc was thirty metres away when the bird turned around and saw it. Same as before the two critters just stopped and stared at each other, and same as before the croc started making that weird gurgling noise. Bird wasn't so hypnotised by it this time though. It squawked real loud and reared up, spreading its wings wide so they sprayed rainbows out in all directions. If that was s'posed to scare the croc it didn't work. It took a hop back, but then started moving forwards again, opening that long snout and showing more teeth than I'd seen in one place before. Glassbird kept its wings out, and every step the croc took the bird took one back. They circled around the clearing like that, keeping that same distance between them; I figured the croc was waiting for the right moment to jump, the bird waiting for its chance to get into the air, but before either of them made their move I got the chance to make mine. Took most of an hour for them to dance a full lap of the clearing so's the bird was back to almost where it started. Almost, but not exactly. This time it was right on the nest, wings still stretched out, still squawking like some deranged chicken. The croc moved in closer, and the glassbird didn't back away this time. Guess it had picked its ground to make a fight of it. Everything stopped. Whole planet went quiet and still. Felt like even the air stopped moving. Then the croc dropped down deep onto its haunches, ready to jump. From what I'd seen I reckoned it could've covered the thirty metres to the nest in one go, easy. I needed to trigger the scrambler right then. I looked down at the remote in my hand, all covered in mud and sweat, and saw my thumb resting on the firing switch, blood running down it from grass cuts on my arms, and I tried to figure why I wasn't pressing that switch. See my head wasn't working right, and when I should've been thinking clear a whole load of crap poured in and muddied everything up. If the scrambler did put the glassbird down then I was just making it easier for the croc. If the croc didn't get it, or me, then could I keep that bird alive and asleep till Daviss arrived with the transport? If I did keep it alive, then how could they ever let it wake up, 'cos soon as it did it would kill itself for sure. And did I even want to keep it alive? Sven had died 'cos of that bird, so shouldn't I be wanting to grind the goddamn thing into powder under my boot? Wouldn't it be worth letting the last glassbird die, just because I could? Can't be many who've had power over a whole species like that. Not the close up and personal kind of power that I had then anyways. Yeah, sure, lots of folks must've killed the last of something before, but I bet they didn't *know* it was the last. It was the knowing that made it buzz like it did. All of that crap arrived in my head at the same time. Took a lot less time to think it than it just did to say it, and the only way I could think to flush it all outta there was to say 'fuck it' and press the switch.

Scrambler didn't make any noise when it fired, but the glassbird did. For a second those crystal feathers all glowed bright blue and a screech came outta its beak like nothing I'd ever heard before. Wouldn't want to hear it again neither. Thought my ears were going to bust. Then it went quiet and just slumped down into the nest. Couldn't tell if it was dead or not, and didn't have time to think on it. The plasma flare was outta my belt and I was running into the clearing, screaming like a banshee to try and scare the croc away. I couldn't even guess at how long a scrambler would keep a glassbird down, so everything was gonna have to happen fast. I'll tell you, after so long having to keep quiet it felt real good to be making that much noise again. When the scrambler had fired the croc had jumped back a ways, trying to figure what had happened with its dumb critter brain. Then I came running out and it had to make a choice. Problem with a dumb critter brain is that when it has to make a choice there are only ever two options, and that dumb critter picked the wrong one. Soon as I saw the way it looked at me, all hate and no fear, I kinda knew that the dumbest critter there was me. First shot from the plasma flare went right under the croc as it took off. Lucky for me we both messed up. I set a tree on fire and the croc put way too much juice into its jump and cleared me by two metres. Guess we were both running on adrenalin. I turned fast and pulled the trigger on the flare again as soon as the croc landed, before it had time to turn and come back at me. Can't say I was too happy when nothing happened. Those plasma flares aren't designed for rapid fire and there's a pre-heat on the igniter that has to get back up to temperature before it's good to go again. Takes about fifteen seconds and I'd only given it about seven of them. Another three for the croc to land and get itself set. I backed away fast, keeping the flare pointed at its head, screaming all sorts of shit to try and keep it thinking. Didn't need to think for long. It charged and then sprang, staying shallow this time, hissing like steam. The flare whined as the igniter came online and I pulled the trigger. A plasma fireball caught the croc on the side of the head, wiping half its face clean off its skull and melting an eye, but that was one tough bastard and it wasn't ready to die yet. Black ooze was pouring outta its head and there was smoking crater where its left eye had been, but all that pain and rage and hate kept coming at me. It had jumped for my neck; the flare had done enough that it only got my right arm, just below the elbow. The bones crumbled like they were chalk and there was pain like nothing I can describe or even want to. We both went down, croc's jaws round my arm, and I was pretty sure that neither of us was ever getting up again. Sounds crazy, don't it? Us lying there in that clearing, stuck together like we were making out, it too weak to do anything but stay clamped on tight, me bleeding to death and not able to move for the pain and the weight pulling down on my messed up arm, all the time knowing that the poison was in me already and in a few hours I'd likely be a puddle of man-shit like old Sven. If I could finish the croc off I might still have a chance, but with my arm stuck down like that I couldn't reach over with my left hand. Tried it and nearly blacked out. Don't' know what I'd have done if I could reach anyways. Didn't have the strength left to lever its mouth open, and that wasn't a throat I'd be able to rip out easy. The flare was a couple of metres away, but it might as well've been back in the transport. Funny the stuff that comes into your head when you give up and wait to die. I suddenly got to thinking about the glassbird waking up and finding me and the croc lying there dead and being pissed about the mess in its clearing. That made me laugh. Always wanted to die laughing. Still do. Turns out that wasn't the day for it though. Outta nowhere I got one of those ideas that you get when you're not trying to have an idea. Up front I was thinking about the glassbird, but something in my back room had carried on thinking about Sven. The way me and the croc were lying meant I could just about lift my right leg over its back, so that's what I did. Then I brought the heel of my boot down hard on its flank. The first two times I reckon it was more painful for me than for the croc 'cos it just sort of grunted and didn't move, but on the third try my boot came down where I wanted, right on top of Sven's hunting knife. It slid in deep, and the croc still had enough life left in it to feel that pain. Seemed right somehow. Guess you could call it Sven's revenge. It made that piggy squeal again and thrashed its tail around, and I felt the grip on my arm lighten up, so I yanked hard and tried to roll away. Hurt like a sonofabitch but I got free. Left a good deal of meat wrapped around the croc's teeth, and from the elbow down my arm looked kinda like somebody had smashed their fist down on a minced beef burrito, but I could move and no amount of pain was going to stop me from crawling over to where the flare was. For the croc? Shit no, I'd given it all the help it needed; it could finish up dying on its own. See I wasn't as dead as I'd figured I was. I'd been poisoned all right, but I guess my arm was messed up so bad that the shit wasn't moving in me fast, and maybe the croc biting down so hard had worked like a tourniquet. I could see it moving in me now though. Dark lines crawled under my skin like worms, working their way up my busted arm, burning like they were hot metal wires. Only one thing to do, so I did it. Picked the flare up with my left hand, jammed the tube hard up into my right armpit and pulled the trigger. Up close and with the end of the tube blocked a plasma flare is a goddamn cannon, and it blew my arm clean off at the shoulder. Don't remember much about the next part, but it's a fair bet that I didn't die from shock. The molten plasma from the flare cauterized my shoulder and stopped the bleeding, and I guess most of the croc's poison must still have been in my arm 'cos I didn't die from that neither. Think I did a lot of puking about then, and when I was done with that I checked on the glassbird. It was still out cold, but alive and in one piece. Took my belt off and strapped its wings down tight to its body, and used the shredded sleeve from the arm that wasn't attached anymore to tie its feet together and its beak closed. That way if it woke up before I did then it wouldn't be able to hurt itself. Can't say how long that took, but I reckon I did it fast as any other man who'd just shot off his own arm could've. Then I blacked out.

Not much more to tell you about what happened on 414. I managed to keep me and that bird alive for the five days till Daviss arrived with the transport, but what I did and when I did it is kinda fuzzy. Doped up on pain meds for most of that time. Kept the bird sedated by mixing the drugs with mashed bugs and leaves and feeding them down its throat with a tube. Did the same for me with the pain meds. Easier to keep mashed bugs down if you don't taste them. Think I must've buried the croc's body, wasn't there when the transport came in. Might have buried what was left of Sven too. Seem to remember doing that. Seem to remember dropping my arm in the hole with him before I filled it in. Rest of the time I slept. Don't think I talked much to Daviss in the transport on the way out, and not spoken to him at all since. Watching Sven die made a mess in his head that will probably never get put straight, and having me in his life ain't going to help any. Saw his sister not long after, and she told me he'd used his cut to open a restaurant in one of the domes on Spinnica. Yeah, we still split the cash three ways, bonus and all. Gave Sven's cut to his kid.

414's been fully colonized awhiles now, so I guess they'll have to give it a name soon or the folks there are going to get to thinking that Central's forgotten about them. Could be they already have named it, but I'll keep with 414 anyhow. Last I heard they were building some big purification plants there. People suddenly started getting sick when they drank the water. Turns out there are too many of those microbes in it now 'cos nearly everything that fed on them or used them to breathe has died. Ain't that something? We find ourselves a new Garden of Eden and we can't even share it with microbes.

Like I said before, they shipped me back to Earth to get the work done on this arm. You like it? Yeah I know there are better prosthetics around these days, but I kinda like this one. So does Melinda. Made me some 'attachments' for it, just for her. Not that she's come calling much since the bonus got spent, but it was good for a while. Real good. When I was in the hospital I got a message from the big eco-dome in Brazil to say that the last glassbird was still alive and looked to be staying that way. Said they'd come up with a drug that kept it calm. Said it was their star attraction. Said they wanted me to name it. How messed up is that? Told them to call it Sven. Got a message back saying the bird was a female and Sven was a boy's name. Told them to go fuck themselves then.

Other thing that came when I was healing was the stuff I'd left in the transport, including all that dreck that Central had given us to read. Was real bored so took to reading it. Mostly crap, just like we knew it was going to be and why we hadn't read it. There were photos too, mostly of the dead stuff they'd collected before we went in after the glassbird. Some of them were kinda creepy, the way those dead animals had been propped up with wire and shit to make them look alive. One of those photos was *real* creepy. Had wire keeping its snout open and some of its teeth were missing, and they'd wired the tail wrong 'cos they had it dragging on the ground instead of held up straight, but they'd managed to get the hate in those black eyes just right. Smaller than the one that took my arm and Sven's life, but still big enough to give me the sweats just looking at it. Then I read the writing underneath, and it made me laugh so much I puked. It said

"Glassbird. Flightless Male. *(Extinct)*."

You're not laughing.

Last CitiXen of Earth

I dreamt about crows again.

I think they were crows. Not really up on birds. Never seen one. Not even a cloned one.

They have a few in the New London reserves but a Suit's salary doesn't run to a ticket to one of those places. I do have databank images of every species that made the cut for Exodus, and the things I'm dreaming about look most like crows. Maybe ravens.

Thousands of them, turning the sky black, filling the air with their grating screams of disapproval. Disapproval and hatred.

Hatred of me.

I can sense it. I can feel it, tearing into me like thousands of razor-sharp talons seeking blood to appease the anger that spurs them ever deeper into my yielding flesh.

Flesh that I can barely remember.

Nice dream, huh? Had it the first time about a week after the drop. Then again about two months after. Then about six weeks after that.

Have it every time I so much as close my eyes now.

It's a malfunction. Must be. Some new type of fucked-up sensory feedback from the dropshell, probably because of the damage it took in the crazy-bitch kick in the balls landing.

I can nearly convince myself of that. Problem is I saw the damned birds before I took the hit, and it was no dream that time.

They appeared with about five minutes of drop-time left. At first I thought passing into atmo had left some sort of pollutant smeared on my optics. But the smear didn't wipe off. It got bigger. It kept getting bigger until I was falling through it, feeling the thumps of those fragile bodies against my shell like somebody was drumming on my brain, nothing but black wings and black eyes filling my vision.

They were there. I saw them. I heard them.

The dropshell didn't.

Nothing on the proximity scope. Nothing on the impact sensors. No motion detected. No sounds recorded.

Which is exactly as it should have been.

There were no crows. There can't have been. This planet couldn't have evolved that fast, and even if it had it couldn't sustain that kind of life.

Now that I come to tell it out loud it just makes me sound crazy. Shit. Guess I'll erase this crap and start again.

Back when I still had flesh on my bones, I worked with a lab tech who fancied himself something of a philosopher. He made a big thing of some old Zen shit that goes "if a tree falls in the forest and there's nobody there to hear it, does it make a sound?" Heard he killed himself couple of years ago, around the time when all the really smart ones started realizing how bad it was going to get. Put on a sixty-foot rope necktie, tied the other end to a bridge support and went for a short full-throttle ride on his bi-speeder. The bike went for about half a mile. He just did the sixty feet.

No idea if anybody heard him do it.

I don't know who you are. I don't know when you are. Hell, for all I know you don't speak English and have no idea what this noise is you're hearing right now.

Doesn't matter.

I'm talking. You're listening. It's enough.

So I thank you for hearing this tree fall.

Thinking on it, there's a good chance this recorder didn't survive the drop. I could just flip it over to playback right now to find out, but all things considered I'd prefer not to know. I'm probably deluding myself believing that this is ever going to get played anyway, so it makes no difference if the recorder is working or not. I choose to believe it works, and therefore it does. Why not? Right here and now, in most important respects, I am God, and God has decided to ignore the shitty little voice in the back of His head telling Him the recorder didn't survive the drop.

Eleven minutes and eleven seconds. According to my chrono, that's how long the descent lasted. Eleven minutes and eleven seconds.

The chrono is capable of recording durations down to a millionth of a second, but I've no idea why they kitted me out with such a top-end piece of tech. Sure, there might be times when that kind of accuracy matters, but take my word for it, clocking a thirty mile fall in a dropshell isn't one of those times. What does matter is firing the dampers at the right time to make for a soft landing. Too early and they run dry when you're still high up and you hit hard. Too late and they don't slow you down enough and you hit hard.

I went for option three. I didn't fire them at all.

Then you hit hardest.

I didn't fire them because something happened in the drop that messed with my head. I was going to tell you about it, but it made me sound like a real nut-job so I erased it.

Dropshells can take the knocks. They're about the toughest shells they make apart from the hardcore military crap they use on the deepers. Dropshells can take the knocks, but a full atmo drop with chutes only and no dampers is asking for trouble, and trouble is what I got. Big trouble.

Not long into atmo I lost a shoulder box. Must have been a weak seal. Happens sometimes; they get brittle when they're superheated and hitting any serious air resistance can pop them right off. Lost most of the stims and neuro-boosters, including my emergency meds. Shouldn't be a problem. I've never shown signs of autocorporeal dysmorphia before and I'm not planning to start now.

If losing that box had been the only glitch on the drop I'd have called that a decent result.

It wasn't.

Right knee joint pretty much exploded on landing and I put a crack in my left side that took my entire supply of fusion polymer to fix. Most excitingly, the electrical overload when my knee blew took out ground nav and communications. All I have left is this recorder and one self-contained emergency data slug.

I was against the dropshell idea from the start. Not so much that they had to fit me into it kicking and screaming, but enough for me to put in a formal objection to the Field Commander in New London. It was 'duly noted', but the fuckers went ahead with the Suit plan anyway. Why not? It was only my life on the line, after all. I guess what really pisses me off is that they were right. A shuttle could make it down, but none of the ones still sturdy enough for a flight in atmosphere could carry enough fuel to reach escape velocity and get back to the colony ship. If things went to plan, they were going to need every airworthy lander they had, so wasting one on a one-way trip made no sense when there were Suits around. Even if there had been atmo-taxis big enough to get back into orbit, they wouldn't have used them.

They couldn't spare the juice.

Not many knew yet, but they soon would. Getting here had emptied the primary tanks and used up most of the reserve. They were already using stuff from the smaller ships to feed The Britannia's main engines. I'd even heard talk of trying to rig up some kind of biowaste injector unit. If you want to know how effective a propulsion system that is, stick on a pair of bladewheels and see how far you can move yourself by farting.

There was talk of sending an androne down, but those things are just too damn twitchy and even the smartest ones can't think for shit when they come up against something they haven't been primed for. There's plenty would say I can't think for shit at any time, but somebody somewhere must believe I think better than an androne. Some said they should just make a few passes with an atmosphere probe. Cheaper and quicker, minimal fuel usage, and high res scans of the surface would be almost as good as coming down. The brass weren't buying that. Samples of the upper atmosphere wouldn't tell them much about conditions on the ground, and you can't do chemical analysis of a photograph no matter how high the resolution. So it came down to two choices: a remote survey lander or a Suit. The survey lander was the obvious choice. They had a fully equipped on-board lab, plus they were remotely controlled so you didn't need to rely on some flaky androne to make your decisions. The downside was that to keep in touch and reduce time lag between commands and responses you needed to stay in geosynchronous orbit, and that took fuel. Fuel they didn't have. The other thing they didn't have was a lander. They started with ten. After dropping four en route the plan was to use five of the remaining six when we got here. First two of those en-route deployments went fine. Third one went haywire halfway through the launch cycle when the lander fired its primary thruster in the hold of the tug that was hauling it. Turned the tug, its crew, and all the other landers into so much glistening space-dust.

I guess my real objection to them sending a Suit was that right from the get-go I knew it would be me they'd be volunteering to send. It had to be me.

It had to be me because I was the only one who was expendable. The only Citixen.

That's c-i-t-i-x-e-n, with an 'x' instead of a 'z'. Most people write the 'x' bigger than the other letters, just to remind us of the significance of it. Me, I write it with a bigger 't', drawn like a cross for them to crucify us on like the fucking martyrs we are.

But now I'm getting ahead of myself.

The reason I'm making this recording is to answer a few simple questions, though answering them is probably more for my benefit than yours.

I'll deal with the least important question first.

Why me?

I've already answered it, but what I said probably makes no sense without some context, so to that end here's a quick history lesson.

For as long as people have been around they've wanted to be around for longer. Prolonging physical life was one of the two big driving forces behind human progress. The other was the quest to create artificial intelligence. By the end of the last millennium, they'd gone as far as they could with living longer. As far as I know the record is still two-hundred and nine years for a pure human. They'd also pretty much given up on trying to create artificial intelligence. They thought they were close a few times, but even the most promising ones ended up running power plants or serving time as on-boards for deep-space factory freighters. They were damn smart alright, but they were no better than androanes when it came to making decisions. No humanity, they said. Humanity was something that they could never programme into a computer, so it could never be more than just a computer. They started worrying that one of these damn smart machines would make a decision that made sense to it but wiped out a city or some shit in the process.

So they stopped trying to put artificial intelligence into machines. They started trying to put real intelligence into them instead. I suppose it made all sorts of sense back then. The line in the dirt that measured how long you lived was drawn by the flesh, not the mind. Drugs could keep the mind going, but nothing could stop the flesh and bones from wearing out. What, then, if you could separate the mind from the flesh? Took them a while to get there because they started from the wrong place. For a long time they thought they could take a consciousness from a person and stick it into some sort of artificial brain box. Do a kind of braindump download into a synthetic neuro-net.

It never worked.

They wanted Socrates. They got psychos, simpletons and suicides. Then they got shelved.

Then some bright spark decided that if the mind couldn't be taken out of the brain, then the brain would have to come with it. Success was a long time coming, but this time it came. A lot of people had their brains fried whilst the scientists were figuring out that there were rules that couldn't be broken. Transplants only worked into machines that mimicked the basic layout of a human body. Transplants only worked for a limited time before the brain had to be moved into a new machine. That was a bitch. Something to do with the mind subconsciously expecting the body to run down and not being able to cope if it didn't. Sometimes that happened in just a few months. Sometimes it took sixty years or more. There was no predicting it. Like I said, that was a bitch.

The final rule was an even bigger bitch. You could only have ten transplants.

Or so they said.

A tech once told me that the ten transplant rule was bullshit. Almost. Sure, there's irreparable synaptic breakdown each time the brain was moved and anywhere from the seventh transplant onwards could be a problem, but an average of ten still allowed for a decent safety margin. It was like those 'eat by' dates they put on nutripacks. The stuff might go bad by then, but most of the time it'd be safe for a good while after. The real reason was money. Suits cost. They have to be DNA prepped months in advance of a transplant. The operation itself takes around seventy-two hours, with three surgical teams of seven on an eight-hour rotation. At least that's how it was at the beginning. For the transplant I just went through I got two teams of five doing twelve-hour shifts. I'm not convinced they even bothered to scrub-up again on the second and third shifts.

Sorry, getting ahead of myself again.

So they managed to spoon human brains into mechanical bodies and not send them insane in the process, but that's when everybody else went insane instead. You don't need to know all the details, which is great because I don't know them either. I just know that the same philosophical shit about the nature of life and the location of the soul gets shoved in our faces even now.

I guess it scared people. We weren't human enough to be called human. We were too human to be called machines.

We called ourselves Suits.

They called us Citizens.

With a 'z'.

It was a name that acknowledged that we were *something*, without having to really nail down what that something was. It was an acceptance that we were part of the state without allocating us a place in it.

For most of us, it was an insult.

They spat it at us, when they weren't actually spitting at us. There were calls to get the Citizen programme shut down before things got too fucked up and somebody got hurt, but by then the genie was well and truly out of the bottle. So 'to keep the peace' they neutered us. We had to agree that all suits be fitted with remote overrides. We had to agree to surrender our veto on transplants so they could stick us into whatever suit they needed us to be in. We had to agree to keeping our helmet visors down permanently when there were wetbags around, just so they could convince themselves that we really were just mechanicals. Humanoid, but not human. Not that different to an automech EVA, or a fire suppression unit with full heat shields. No sir, nothing scary or weird to see here.

Even those early Suits didn't need to breathe as such and could handle temperature extremes at both ends, so we could do drops into 'unfavourable' environments, and underwater work. We could even do exterior hull repairs and engine baffle clearances without ships needing to skindock. Some of the bigger ships didn't even need to slow down 'cos a Suit's magclaw stayed attached even in gravity. Usually.

Suits were useful on long hauls as well. Easier and cheaper to put into stasis and take out again at short notice because there was less organic material to worry about. Of course, faster and more frequent freezes and thaws meant more chance of getting ice crystals forming in your brain and leaving you with a single-digit I.Q, but the pay was good. Sorry, that's an old Suit joke. Back then, Suits didn't get paid. We weren't crew or employees.

We were equipment.

For a while we took it. Took it right in the shitter.

Dinah changed all that.

There's not a Suit operating today old enough to have met Dinah Rakowski, but there's plenty claim they did. She was the first female Suit. Came into the programme after a bomb took out her security station on one of those huge Titan orbiters. The same bomb killed her husband and the child inside her. The explosion ripped her to pieces and that blast just kept on going til it knocked the Citizen programme onto its butt. Not just because she was a woman. She was also the first Suit not to be ex-military. She was law enforcement, and volunteer law enforcement at that. Not that you could tell any of that when you saw her. She was a Suit, and looked like every other Suit. It's not like they gave her armoured carbon-fibre breasts or a pastel-pink paintjob or any shit like that, but when people looked at her they didn't see what they saw when they looked at other Suits. Part of that might have been because of her voice. Suits don't have any external markings - there's no label on the outside to identify the contents of the tin - but we do get to keep our own voices. Well, synthesized versions of them anyway, compiled from our vo-tag idents. They didn't like doing it but they had to: it was something to do with the brain's need for consistent self-identity across transplants. So individual voices we could have, just not a collective one. Maybe hearing a female voice coming out of a hunk of titanium and carbon-fibre did more than impact on the ears. Maybe it opened eyes too. Whatever the reason, for the first time since the start of the Citizen programme, wetbags were able to see beyond the machine. The people saw a fellow person. The programme saw a PR goldmine. Would you believe they even got her doing talk shows? It was a talk show host on one of the big networks that got a bit too pally with Dinah. Called her a Dress. She wasn't the first to do it – hell, some of the other Suits called her that when she wasn't around – but this was the first time anybody had done it when Dinah was there to hear it. It was meant to be funny. Just a throwaway line to warm-up the audience. The woman probably wished she'd thrown that line away sooner when Dinah gave her face a little tickle. Shattered her jaw and cheekbone, and it all happened so fast that Dinah's section chief didn't get to the remote quick enough to stop Dinah's fist from connecting. The fact that he got to it at all probably stopped that punch from taking the woman's head clean off her shoulders.

You'd think that a live broadcast of so much physical strength attached to so little anger management would have played right into the hands of the anti-Citizen brigade, and you'd be right to think it. It gave them a trump card, but they never got to lay it down. Before the shit had finished flying off the fan, Dinah disappeared. She turned up again a few days later on a vidlog that got posted on the Net. It showed her walking up to the edge of the roof of a skyscraper in New London and then going over like some wind-up toy tipping off a table. It was over two-hundred storeys down. If she'd been in a dropshell or combat hull she'd have made it no problem. Two-hundred storeys isn't much more than a big step for some Suits. Dinah was in a UA-33. Urban assistance. Built for speed and agility.

Great for running down a food thief but not worth a damn when it comes to impact resistance.

The vidlog only showed Dinah walking about ten yards or so before going over the edge. She walked ten yards, the vid ran for nine hours.

Baby steps.

For nine hours, Dinah Rakowski took the tiniest fucking baby steps up to the edge of that building, and for every second of those nine hours she wouldn't have been able to think about shit except that she was going to die.

The wetbags said it was suicide and barely investigated it.

The Suits said like fuck it was suicide and investigated it themselves.

They knew where to start that investigation. The speed the enquiry into Dinah's death was wrapped barely paid lip-service to what the law was supposed to be about. Somebody had pulled strings, and they'd have to be fucking long strings to reach far enough to produce that kind of high-profile ignorance.

Turned out the strings weren't just long, they went damn near all the way to the top. The Commander of the Titan fleet had arranged the 'terrorist' bombing on Dinah's ship when she started sniffing the stink of a shitload of dirty cash that was heading his way. He probably thought he was finished when Dinah survived the explosion, but the trauma of being reborn as a Suit screws around with your memories like you wouldn't believe. Some wake up the first time thinking they'd *literally* just been born. After her initial transplant,

Dinah's memory loss was pretty much total. Thing is, as your brain adjusts to the new set-up, those gaps in your memory start filling up again. Sooner or later, Dinah was going to remember who it was tried to kill her. Before that could happen, the bastard in question got in touch with his fifteen-year-old daughter and 'persuaded' her to whore herself out to the husband of the chat show host. The self-same chat show host that Dinah assaulted. Then daddy dearest blackmailed the stupid schmuck into getting his wife to provoke Dinah into attacking her. He also told him exactly which button his wife would need to push. The wife played along because being attacked by a Suit during a live broadcast would put her career on steroids. Excruciatingly painful reconstructive facial surgery was a small price to pay for that, apparently.

So why go to all that trouble just to get Dinah to take a swing at a nothing chat show host?

That was the bit that took the longest to figure out.

The first reason was to try and turn the populace away from Dinah. Give them a reason to hate her. Discredit her, if you like. It would make her supposed suicide easier to swallow.

The second reason was to get Dinah's section chief to use the shell remote to try and pull Dinah's punch.

Thing about a shell remote, they said, is that the encryption is unbreakable, and the signal itself, they said, is impossible to clone. Except that was all just horseshit. Commander Shithead-Fuckwit – that wasn't his real name, in case you're wondering, but those guys always have polished-brass shotgun names so my version will do fine – had access to some top-end military tech. He got some of that tech close to Dinah inside a trick camera, set up to decrypt and clone any undecryptable, uncloneable signal it detected in the frequency range they used for shell remotes. Then all he needed to do was get Dinah up onto that roof. Nobody has figured out exactly how he did it, but there were reports of a child's screams coming from that roof about twelve hours before the timestamp on the vidlog. Suits can't scream, so it wasn't Dinah. Most reckon that whoever did the screaming was the Judas goat that lured Dinah up there. They also reckon it was Commander Shithead-Fuckwit's daughter again. They didn't reckon that right away, but a couple of months later when they found most of her clogging the workings of a sewer pump they started reckoning it.

Guess daddy didn't like loose ends.

Once Dinah was up on that roof, all he needed to do was walk her right off it and he'd have his nice, neat suicide. People might have believed it too.

People might have. But back then, Suits weren't people. A group of them tried to get hold of Dinah's black box, but it was 'requisition denied, case closed, no further action required'. Or 'fuck off' for short.

So they broke into a secure facility and took it. Nothing's that secure against a bunch of pissed-off Suits. Then they went public with what they found.

The black box proved that Dinah stepped off that roof because of a signal from a remote. It also proved that she fought every tiny step of the way. It should have been impossible, or at least the shell designers had always thought it was, but Dinah managed to push back against the remote control. Each time it tried to move her leg forward, she pulled it back by sheer effort of will. The box recording showed every servo-muscle getting a constant stream of conflicting commands, the neurotriggers firing at a speed way beyond what a normal human brain should have been able to generate. It was a staggering display of mental strength and control from a woman who knew that she was about to die, because for all of that strength and control she was still moving forward. Agonizingly slowly, but still forward.

That fight was never about staying alive; Dinah was just buying as much time as she could. Time to speak.

Time to tell.

Seems her memory loss wasn't as total as she'd made it out to be. She'd just needed to wait until Commander Shithead-Fuckwit made his move. She needed something to tangle him up in that he wouldn't be able to grease his way out of, and she worked out early that her own death would be that something. As far as she was concerned, she was on borrowed time anyway.

For the whole of the nine hours she was fighting, she was talking. Talking about the evidence she'd collected before they tried to kill her. Talking about the recordings she'd made of the conversations between Commander Shithead-Fuckwit and the chat show host's husband. Talking about how Suits should have the same rights as wetbags. Talking about the husband and child she had lost.

Not everything she said made sense – the strain of fighting the remote began to tell after a few hours, and near the end there was more emotion than logic – but the actual words didn't matter. The very fact that there *was* emotion was what mattered. People knew that Suits could get angry, Dinah's punch had shown them that. Her last words showed them that Suits could feel much more, and that hit them much harder than any punch. It had been so much easier for them when we were anonymous and emotionless. Now they had to deal with us being able to feel love, fear, loss and remorse with the same passion as they did.

Dinah also showed them that we could die.

We were more than machines. Machines get shut down; you have to be alive to die.

They didn't like it. They didn't like it, but they dealt.

Billions of humans have died over the centuries, and nearly all of those deaths were meaningless. Dinah Rakowski was the first operational Suit to die, and that one death had more meaning than even she could have imagined it would.

Within a year there were laws giving Suits, and any Biomech scoring more than a seven on the Turing scale, rights of their own. Remotes were banned, and Suits were given three vetoes, each one allowing them to refuse any transplant for two years. *Any* transplant, including the ones they needed to keep them alive. It was government sanctioned suicide but nobody kicked up a stink about it because the grudging acceptance of our existence didn't extend to giving a shit if we decided to off ourselves. In return for the vetoes, and the hard-won 'article sixteen', the ten-transplant guideline became an unyielding rule. Article sixteen restricted the type of shell we could be dumped into on our final transplant. It might not sound like a big deal, but not ending your days in a malfunctioning heap of rusty junk was a big fucking deal to us.

Less than six months after we got rights, we got means. Suits started getting paid. Until then, we'd just worked for our keep and if we died we were just scrap. Now we were allowed to own shit. We got life insurance. Health care. Servicing. Funerals. The whole nine yards and then some.

We thought we were being so clever when we were being so incredibly fucking dumb.

Yes, Suits had rights now. *Suits* rights, not human rights. By giving us exactly what we thought we wanted, they got exactly what *they* wanted. In our push to be the treated the same, we had all but demanded laws that proved we were different.

The Bill of Citizens' Rights was also the first time we'd been called Citizens on something official. 'Til then it had just been another piece of shit to be thrown at us. Turns out shit sticks.

They managed to keep the ten-transplant rule a secret for a while, but it was too important to stay that way. Important to us, at least. Once the news was out a new name appeared for Citizens on their tenth and final transplant. Always thought it was strange that so many of them knew what the Roman numeral for ten was when none of them had any fucking clue what a Roman was.

It was around that time we took to calling them wetbags.

Because when you're a species desperately clinging to existence by your bleeding fingernails it makes a whole lot of sense to start calling each other stupid fucking names. Guess that's why we were in such a mess to begin with.

History lesson over. Back to the question.

I got my first shell in September 247 P.E.

This dropshell is my tenth. Today is the fifteenth – no, sixteenth - of March, 692 P.E. The maths I'll leave to you. All I know is I'm old. Too damn old.

I'm finding it particularly funny today that we still use the same 365 day year for the Post Exodus calendar as we did before. Funny, because I never got to live on a planet with a 365 day year, but now I get to die on one.

Yay for me.

Thing is, article sixteen says that you can refuse a dropshell for your final transplant. Dropshells mean drops. Drops are real dangerous. Shitty thing to do to a Suit for their last transplant. Not that it never happens. Heard plenty of stories of Suits going to sleep in their tip-loader or plate-welder and waking up in a dropshell. Already dropping.

That's one of those things they tell you doesn't really happen. Like 'repurposed' used shells. That doesn't happen either. All transplants have to be sanctioned and only 'approved' recipients can become

Suits. Yeah right. Like there isn't a line of rich old farts out there who won't give every penny they have to get a few extra years of life in a shell that was DNA coded for somebody else. Shells can't be recoded they say. It's impossible, they say. Like money can't buy the impossible.

Apart from the actual drop, a dropshell is a pretty damn good choice for a CitiXen. They're big and solid. Built to last. Top-of-the-line radiation and particle shielding, multiple duracharge power cells, sealed-unit titanium joint bearings and solid fuel landing thrusters. You can be damn sure with a dropshell that the hardware is going to last longer than the meat inside it.

Other thing is, I had a veto left. I could have refused the transplant even if I didn't have article sixteen to hide behind.

Like I said; too damn old.

Old, and the only Nine on board The Britannia. There were two Sevens and an Eight, but nobody else lined up to be a CitiXen. One of the Sevens, Ayanna, had already used all of her vetos. She had family still alive, and the ones with family are always the first to run out of vetoes. She was in her twenties when she got her first suit. Her great-great-granddaughter just had her hundred-and-fifty-second birthday.

The other Seven, O'Hara, had a stasis heater fail on him after the last long haul. Since then he's been wrong. Nothing you can exactly put your finger on. Just …wrong.

Chen, the Eight, was an arsehole.

Ayanna would have taken the mission because she had to. She wouldn't have wanted it but you could have trusted she'd do it right.

O'Hara won't get another transplant. They won't trust new hardware to damaged meat, so the poor bastard is going to spend the rest of his days as an asteroid miner. They won't put damaged meat back into a freezer either, so he's going to spend the rest of his days as an asteroid miner with no asteroids to mine.

Chen was a showboater. He'd have taken the mission because he wanted it, and then he'd have fucked it up.

Where was I? I had the crow dream again. No, wait, I erased that, didn't I? I'll restore it. Probably going to screw up the start of this recording for you but you're going to have to live with it.

It was different this time. No swarms of black wings filling the sky. Just one bird. A single black emissary, here in my cave. Just one bird. A big one. Not ten feet away, standing in the shadows at the edge of the glow from the lumipack. I didn't even realize I'd fallen asleep, but that's happening a lot now. I drift in and out.

Did I tell you that already?

Like with the other dream, it's more what I feel than what I see that stays with me.

Before there was hate and anger.

This time there's curiosity. I'm being studied. Scrutinized. This creature that can't exist is checking me out.

I'm so damned tired.

I think I've wasted enough breath on 'why me?', so I'm moving on. The second question is 'why now?'.

That's the one with the shortest answer.

Now, because it's now or never. Humanity is all but done. Since Exodus we've been clinging to the edge of a precipice, unable to find a solid foothold in the universe. We've become nomads, scattered through space looking for a planet to call home. Go back a few centuries and there was talk about terraforming any planet we found that came close, That's all it was. Talk. Atmosphere processing was way beyond our capabilities, but without it we were screwed. There were plenty of bases dotted around on those 'planets that came close' and the colony ships had thriving populations, but there was a disease infecting those bases and ships that was going to end us as a species.

A disease called hope.

Hope that we would eventually get terraforming to work.

Hope that there would be no more failures like there had been at Mars Base just after Exodus, or the disaster that was the first attempt at a settlement on Titan. Then there was the fiasco on New Eden. That one really hurt. A planet with a breathable atmosphere that was already life sustaining and we couldn't live there. Not only could we not live there, three-hundred and twenty five thousand of us died there. Since we threw ourselves out into space we'd been dreading the day when we ran into a huge killer alien. When we finally did run into that killer alien, it was microscopic.

Hope that one of the deepers would finally find a planet with a breathable atmosphere.

See the problem with hope is that it stops a man getting desperate, and if there's one thing we should be right now it's desperate. If the people knew the truth then there would be panic, and that's why they haven't been told. Eleven of the sixteen deepers are gone, either destroyed or out of contact for so long they've been classed as lost. The colony ships are hopelessly beyond repair and they're all going to suffer some kind of catastrophic failure sooner rather than later. All of the bases are on borrowed time. Not only is there no chance of atmosphere processing ever working on the kind of scale we'd need to terraform, the raw materials needed to keep the air scrubbers running at the bases we have is in short supply. The people who do know all that – the important people in New London – did get desperate. That's why The Britannia was sent here. It's the ultimate act of desperation, and it's taken over a hundred years to perform it. That's how long it's been since that desperate decision was taken.

Doesn't take a genius to work out that if we were in the shit over a hundred years ago, we're in it much deeper now.

We're the first ship to come here since Exodus, and our being here is another of those things that it's best 'the people' don't know about. There are at least a dozen fundamentalist, Terraphile or religious groups that would raise a stink. Some of those groups have been known to use high explosives to get stinky with.

Last night I met a man who wasn't there.

He didn't say much. Or anything.

I was watching the crow. It was in the same place as before, right at the edge of the reach of the lumipack, keeping to the shadows. I was watching it watching me.

Then I had an idea. Seems I have to be dreaming to get a good idea these days.

I turned the power output down a couple of notches on the lumi, shrouding the bird in darkness. After a minute or two it reappeared on the edge of the smaller circle of light, just far enough out of the dark for me to see its black eyes fix on me.

Then I turned the lumi back to full power.

The circle of light expanded faster than the bird could react.

Only what my smart idea had managed to catch wasn't a bird anymore. Squatting down on his haunches in the sickly sodium-yellow light of the lumipack, staring at me with the bird's black eyes, was a man. Long hair, long beard, filthy clothes worn almost to nothing. A mess of a man, but a man. Fucker was wearing blue jeans too. It would have taken a year's salary and some heavy black market contacts for me to get a pair of them to slide my ass into, back when my ass wasn't a titanium reinforced carbon fibre tow hitch.

Even those jeans were faded and worn through at the knees. The only thing about this man that looked new were his boots.

No, not *his* boots. *My* boots.

Back before I was a Suit, I saw those boots in a vintage store on one of the colony ships. Black leather, white stitching. They were labelled as 'cowboy boots, real leather, probably 23rd century, original vac-seal packaging so perfect condition'. Even after all this time as a Suit I can remember exactly what those boots looked like and what it said on the sale ticket.

I didn't know what 'cowboy boots' were, but I knew I wanted them. I wanted them so much it made my guts hurt. Knowing that I would never have them didn't make me want them any less. No shuttle jockey ever owned boots like those. Hell, I wasn't even a spacer, my licence only covered in-ship hops. Even after I was fitted for my first Suit I didn't stop thinking about those damn boots. About the time I got my third Suit they made stuff made from real leather, even the old stuff, illegal.

Don't think this guy cares.

Guess it was a bit of a knee-jerk reaction, but I went for the compact forced-plasma pistol strapped to my left thighpod. As far as I know, there's no such thing as a compact forced-plasma pistol, so I shouldn't have been pissed about the fact that there wasn't one strapped to my thighpod, but it was my dream so if I wanted a fucking plasma pistol there should have been a fucking plasma pistol.

The man caught the movement of my hand going to my leg and he smiled. For just a second I thought he was going to speak to me.

Then he was gone.

I've having trouble concentrating now. Not sure if what's in my head is the stuff I was planning to tell you or the stuff I've already told you.

I'm pretty sure I told you about the landing and my knee giving out. Got to say I was one lucky son of a bitch really. Landed in deep sand. Took the edge off the impact and created a molten silicon plug over a power cell with buckled shielding that was pissing out something nasty. There were a couple of big rock formations not fifty metres away. If I'd come down on either of those I'd have been history. Not even a dropshell could have survived that. The initial impact in the sand temporarily overloaded every damn system I had, including me, and I guess I blacked out. That was a first.

When I found my way back from la-la land I was in a cavern under a pile of rock and sand. I say cavern but the place wasn't natural. Definitely man-made. Some kind of transport system using rails and tunnels.

I did what I could with the knee, but the damage was more than a field repair could put right. I managed to deal with the crack in the shell's side plating and ditch the leaking power cell. The comms being u-s was no biggie. If I couldn't fix the transmitter, I still had the slug. I was supposed to stay dark for as long as possible anyway because the drop hadn't been sanctioned yet. All that political crap just gets in the way of getting the job done.

The job.

Survey. Analyse. Report. Watch. Wait.

Survey the surface topography and any structures in the vicinity of the designated drop zone.

Analyse soil, water and atmospherics.

Report on viability of establishing self-sustaining colony.

Watch my report get tossed in the trash no matter what I say because a full scale colonization landing is going to happen anyway. We have no choice.

Wait until a 'scouting expedition' pays me a friendly visit because I'm going to be about as loose as a loose end gets.

They know I'll have worked all that out. They'll also know that I'll have worked out that the only way I get a happy ending here is to send them exactly the report they need me to.

What they don't know is what it means to be a CitiXen. It means that we've already got to the ending, and we don't give a shit how happy it is. I decided before I came that they were going to get the truth, and to hell with what they thought about it or what they'd do to me. The truth, whether they liked it or not.

Didn't take me long to work out they weren't going to like it and I was going to get my happy ending after all.

I'm not sure how long it's been since my last recording. The sun doesn't reach down here and my chrono is smashed. Don't remember how that happened, just found the pieces. Looks like somebody took a rock and beat the crap out of it.

Definitely something fucked up in my head. My memories are corrupting. I've been trying to think back to tell you what I found out after the drop, but what I'm remembering now isn't the way it happened then.

Because now *he's* there.

It's impossible to explain. Don't even know where to start, it's that crazy. All I know is that until I dreamt him in this cavern, you know, the dream I told you about where he started out as a bird and then turned into a man, I'd never seen him before. Never seen anybody like him. Now when I try to remember anything from before that dream, he's there.

He's always there.

Yea, I know. And I was worried that telling you I had a dream about crows was going to make me sound like a nut-job.

This grubby longhaired stranger in a sleeveless red shirt, blue jeans and black leather cowboy boots was at my ninth birthday party.

And every other birthday party I can remember.

He was at my father's funeral.

My first day at flight school.

The day I signed my brain over to the Citizen programme.

Always there. Always the same. Even the same age, no matter how old the memory I find him in. And he's in all of them. Sometimes he's standing beside the person I was talking to. Sometimes he's lurking in the background. Sometimes I just catch him in my peripheral vison.

For a while I thought my fondest memory – my first teenage fumble-fuck with Tanya Marcus the day before I left for flight school – had escaped contamination. Then I see him, reflected in the glass of the photo of Tanya's husband beside her bed. He's smiling at me.

No, he's *grinning* at me.

I know how fucked up all this sounds. Trust me, it doesn't sound any less fucked up to me than it does to you.

I collected the first water samples about three weeks after the drop. It took me that long to reach the sea. It was supposed to have taken one day at most, but then both knee joints were supposed to be working. Following one of the tunnels in my cavern led me into a transit structure with stairs leading up to what might once have been the surface. Had to dig my way out through eighty feet of sand and rubble to get to where the surface was now. Whatever had been here before had been lost to this new desert like a wound that had healed without leaving so much as a scar.

I call it a new desert, but it's more likely to be an old desert that's moved. They say the impact winter lasted ninety years, but there was no new ice age. For the first few years there was no sun but light everywhere as everything burned. When the sun did come back, the new weather and wind patterns had already started to reshape the planet. More of the sun's heat and radiation makes it down to the surface now, so this planet was never going to be the ice-ball that many had expected us to be coming back to.

When I reached the ocean, I remember seeing the man in my boots standing by the water's edge a few hundred yards away. I know he wasn't really there, I just remember it that way. He was staring out to sea. He didn't look at me, I didn't acknowledge him. That's one of the ways I know these memories are screwed up. If I'd been collecting samples and really seen a person there with me I'd sure as hell have reacted.

I also know that I was going to avoid taking a closer look at the rockier part of the beach because it didn't look like a smart place to walk for a one-legged Suit. Then something made me change my mind and head across the sand to where the sea sucked at a field of rocks and boulders, defining the boundary between land and water that stretched from where I stood to somewhere beyond the range of my opticals. Some of it looked more uniform and porous, perhaps the remains of structures or highways. At the time I thought it was dumb luck that I found the crawling thing. Now my head is telling me that *he* led me to it. There he is, squatting on a boulder, pointing at the water-filled depression at its base. That's where the crawling thing was. It was grey-brown in colour and almost invisible against wet sand, so I didn't see it until it moved. That crawling thing had no more right to be there than the man in my boots. It was small, maybe three or four mil long, and slow-moving. I scooped it into a breather jar, along with some water and sand, and put it into the sample pod. As I did, I saw another of them in the water. I dipped another breather jar into the pool and lifted it up to the light. There must have been twenty of them swimming in the clear water. And they weren't grey, they were almost completely transparent, living prisms that created tiny flashes of colour as they moved. They could move quicker in water, so I guess they had evolved to swim rather than crawl. Course, they shouldn't have evolved at all. There wasn't supposed to be anything alive here, they'd made that clear before the drop. It was impossible. So impossible that they hadn't given me the kit to do any serious analysis of organic life. According to them I was going to see a ghost world; a legacy of crumbling edifices and decaying monuments remembering a past I knew nothing about. If I'm honest with you, it was a past I didn't give a shit about to begin with. I guess you'd call that ironic.

Now I think on it, perhaps there's even more irony to my saying I didn't give a shit when I haven't done one since before I became a Suit. Suit's don't need to shit. The few nutrients my meat needs don't produce any significant waste product. Once every six months or so there might be enough in the lube filters to compress into a small bale of organic and inorganic waste, but I'd hardly call that taking a shit.

I'm wandering again.

There's plenty who still call this place 'home', though none of them have seen anything except old pictures and movies about how it used to be before one mother of a hunk of rock ripped the planet a new one.

Since Exodus there have been those who would kill to come back here and those who would die to stop them from trying. I've always been able to see both sides of the argument, and I've always been able to ignore them both equally. Recently that's been tougher. The religious nuts who say that we should never come back here have been making noises, trying to drown out the talk of having no options except coming back. Some of those noises have been very loud bangs.

I've stopped dreaming. The man in my boots has gone, and the crows have gone with him. It's been a week since I've seen him, and he's gone from my memories as well. I don't know if that is a good thing or not. He's never spoken or responded to any of my questions, but his presence in my head has meant that I wasn't alone. Now he's gone my only companions are a billion years of evolution away from being up for a conversation.

At least not dreaming seems to be making me less tired when I'm awake. Went through a bad patch for a while and I'm going to have to work harder to keep all these minor systems failures on the dropshell becoming one major one, but for the moment at least I seem to be on the up.

The data slug is ready. Everything has taken longer than I thought it would, but I'm not at my best. I'm having intermittent power failures and two of my solar rechargers are on the fritz now. How long things have taken I can't even guess at without the chrono. For a while I tried to track the passage of days using the sun but surface temperature and light levels are too much for a Suit without full radiation shielding and optical suppressors. It's a flaw in the dropshell that nobody saw coming. They were designed for short missions by guys who lived their whole lives in low gravity under artificial light. Everything outside this cavern is too damn hot and too damn bright, and the constant fight against a full dose of gravity is wearing the joint servos. This isn't like the place I woke up in. This is a natural cave, and the entrance is big enough to give me working light levels in here without the burning brightness.

I've surprised myself by choosing to spend so much time in this cavern. I've found the remains of structures all around here, some of them tall enough to reach up out of the shifting sands, defying this planet's relentless efforts to be rid of them. I could easily have used one of those places as a base for my work and saved myself some walking. Given the state of my knee and the condition of the shell's primary servos it would have made sense to cut out some unnecessary travel, but I chose not to.

I chose not to because of the ghosts.

I hadn't anticipated the ghosts.

Grey and cold like the buildings they inhabit, they watch me from every empty window. I can remember those windows without the man in my boots invading the memory now, but the ghosts remain. I wasn't lying to you when I said I didn't give a shit about the past, but that doesn't mean I can just forget that nine billion people died here.

In my dream, a thousand crows tried to rip me apart.

When I'm awake, nine billion pairs of eyes judge me. Nine billion croaking voices beg to know why I'm alive and they're not.

Fuck that. I preferred the crows.

Nobody up there on the ship is going to like the report I've put on the slug. It's definitely not the rubber stamp on the colonization plan that they were hoping for. See my new little friends here in these breather jars aren't shrimp, they're flies. Big fat juicy black flies in humanity's ointment. The best analysis I could do with the gear I have was enough to explain the anomaly with the air.

Hold up, I didn't tell you about the air yet, did I? I know I was going to, but I think that was the morning after I met the man in my boots for the first time and I didn't do a recording 'til I was less freaked.

Okay, right, so, the air.

The upper atmosphere sample I got during the drop was what I was expecting to find. High levels of carbon dioxide but not as bad as it had got to before Exodus. Improving oxygen levels as I came down, just about breathable by the time I started seeing birds. That was better than expected. The nanoplankton in the oceans would have been destroyed by the acid rain from the increased nitrogen levels, and even though the ozone layer seems to have survived, albeit as a thinner one than before, the increased ultraviolet levels would have killed those smaller organisms that managed to survive the impact winter. Without that photosynthesis there would have been a big drop in oxygen levels, so finding a breathable atmosphere is as good a start to the mission as I could have hoped for. Didn't take any more samples until after I dug my way out of the transport tunnels.

That's when things stopped making sense.

The ground level sample had much higher concentrations of hydrogen and carbon monoxide than it should. Not only was it not breathable, it was toxic. At first I thought it was bad air seeping from the tunnels, but it was bad everywhere and worst near the ocean. Even now I know why, I still can't make sense of the readings I got during the drop. Hydrogen and c-o levels at higher altitudes were as expected. Certainly nothing to suggest there would be poisonous levels down on the ground.

It's an itch I can't scratch yet.

I can explain where the gases are coming from, but I can't explain how they've become so concentrated so quickly or why they don't appear higher in the atmosphere.

One thing's for sure: after they see my data they won't be sending any shuttles down. There are gas pockets all over the place that would make a landing impossible. Hydrogen and oxygen are volatile bedfellows, but they'd probably stay quiet and asleep unless somebody woke them up with, say, a shuttle engine. Then we'd all be fucked.

So nobody's coming to visit me. They could send another Suit or a breach glider I suppose, but what would be the point? This is just another planet that would need domes for them to live on.

Now that is funny. We come back to Terra just to find out it needs terraforming.

Which brings me back to the big black flies in my breather jars.

You see these little critters are changing Earth's hydrologic cycle, and with it, they're changing the atmosphere. From what I can work out, when they respire in water they release hydrogen in its gaseous form, but the ones that I've found on land are taking in hydrogen and excreting water. There would be no reason for a lifeform that evolved on earth to respire that way, so my guess would be that these things arrived on the rock that killed all of the indigenous life. With no competition they must have thrived and grown in number exponentially, which makes them resilient and adaptable little suckers. If they'd survived in space then maybe they could have survived the impact-winter. It sounds feasible, but there are things that don't add up. These soft-bodied forms would never have survived in space or made it through an atmosphere burn. They could only have got here as microbes, buried deep in the rock, but even allowing for their planetary domination I can't figure how they've evolved into these complex multi-cell organisms so fast and changed the atmosphere so much in just a few hundred years.

But in the end, what I don't know doesn't change what I do know, and what I do know will be enough to stop any thoughts of colonizing this place. We've come home, and the new tenants have changed the locks. They're the earthlings and we're the aliens now.

Personally, I think that's fair. The big rock that finally ended everything wasn't our fault, but we'd already blown it by then anyway. The only reason that there's anybody left at all is because we were already out in space looking for alternatives to a planet we'd bled dry, polluted and over-populated with a supreme display of arrogant denial.

That sounds like a rant. It isn't. Like I said, I don't give a shit about this planet's past: I'm just glad that its future doesn't belong to us.

I'll activate the slug tomorrow, once I'm sure all the data is safely on there. Then I guess I find out just how long a Suit can survive without a transplant. My guess is longer than my brain can survive without food. I still have enough stimpacks to last six or seven months, perhaps longer if I run close to starvation levels, and if I scavenge a few parts from the useless comms system and the smashed chrono I might be able to fix the u-s solar chargers, but I'll still be dead within a year.

Never did find out how that chrono got smashed.

Just another unanswered question that doesn't need answering anymore. Still, it'll give me something to think about as I wait to die.

A year. That's about the same warning as the ghosts got before the rock hit. I've never really given much thought to the afterlife, but wherever the nine billion who died here went, I hope there's room for one more.

Pleased to meet you, hope you know my name.

Sorry, old reference, doubt anybody would get it these days.

Just call me Stan. Though not *the* Stan.

That was a joke, by the way. Thought I'd best mention that in case you didn't notice it, I'm out of practice.

Sorry again. I seem to be having a bit of a head-rush at the prospect of having somebody to talk to. Admittedly that somebody is just an electronic recording device at the moment, but eventually it will be you, and at the risk of freaking you out I feel compelled to add that I know who you are, where you are and what you're wearing right now as you listen to my voice.

His name was David. David Stainsbridge. I don't think it ever told you that. It might get around to it later, but as far as I can tell it's not planning to make any more recordings. Seems it's a little down on the idea that it's going to die.

I have to say, I find that perplexing.

You see, David Stainsbridge has been dead a very long time. This lumbering mechanical thing *thinks* it's David, but it's not. Never was.

I know. I've looked.

I've been through every memory. Every thought. Every line of code.

You know, there's some interesting stuff going on in there. There are memories in there that have become so far detached from the main core that they can't be accessed by the machine.

None of what I found is David Stainsbridge though.

I can't say I completely understand everything I've seen. Machines and computers really aren't my thing.

Too cold.

Soulless.

I much prefer the flesh.

There was flesh in the machine once. I can still feel the echoes of it. Taste them. But they are only echoes. David Stainsbridge did visit for a while, then he moved on. After they transplanted him in to this machine, an accident damaged one of the legs at the knee. They swapped out the leg, and it happened again. It turned out to be a problem with the artificial nervous system miscommunicating commands from the brain. In essence, the machine was constantly ripping its own knee apart as it tried to walk.

It was too big a job for a repair, so they transplanted David Staindbridge out into a different machine.

Something got left behind though.

Nothing physical. I'm not talking about a sliver of brain stuff or a strand of nerve. Essence. That would be a good word for it. It shouldn't have been able to happen. The machine was faulty. Something went wrong when it was manufactured.

If it was a living thing you'd call it a mutation.

And excuse the biology 101, but mutation the key mechanism for evolution.

The machine had evolved. Not artificial intelligence; borrowed intelligence. It was a repository for a man's memories, and therefore it was the man.

Did I lose you there?

Then let me put it this way.

We are each of us a product of our experiences, yes? And those experiences are stored within us as memories. So doesn't it follow that if somebody else is given those memories believing them to be their own, they will retrospectively experience the same events? Accepting that we are all the sum of our life experiences, would those experiences add up to the same sum if we run them through a different calculator?

The answer, it would seem, is yes.

David Stainsbridge was part of this machine long enough for its data storage matrix to replicate David's memories and duplicate his thought processes. Why these engrams were created I can't say. I'd like to think it was a deliberate act of self-preservation by a new lifeform coming to terms with its own existence, and more interestingly, its mortality. I'd like to think that, but it's probably not true. It could just have been faulty wiring.

Still, however dull the cause, the effect was most interesting. When the man was transplanted, the machine went into shock. It became dormant, rejecting any attempts to restart it or install a new mind to control it. As nobody understood what was happening they scrapped it and put it into storage for recycling.

Then the ship blew up.

Massive explosion. I saw it from down here.

I know what you're thinking, but it had nothing to do with me. Yet again, it was mass murder in *his* name. My only bad was not intervening, but when his followers want to blow something up, who am I to interfere? I've never been able to get a handle on it really. He's the one that gets his kicks out of sending plagues and floods, but I'm the bad guy? I'd best not get started down that road or we'll be here all night.

David Stainsbridge died in the explosion. So did everybody else. There were no survivors. Most of the debris from the ship burnt up as it passed through the atmosphere. Great show. I lay back with a cold one and a bucket of nachos to watch. The only things that made it down were the things designed to.

One of those things woke up on the way down.

When it did, it woke up as David Stainsbridge. In a microsecond it had rationalized its predicament. It was supposed to be dropped into the atmosphere, so that must be what was happening.

It intrigued me, so I took a closer look at it as it fell. I did it as crows. Force of habit, I'm afraid. I hadn't done it for a while, and it felt really good if I'm honest.

I also quite enjoyed the sense of fear and confusion I could taste in the air as it fell. The terror of falling from the heavens. Now that I can identify with.

It blamed the crows for not using its rockets to lessen the impact of the fall. That was more rationalization. The rockets hadn't been fuelled. Why should they be, when he machine wasn't going to be dropped?

For a machine it was already doing a fine job of being human. It was even lying to itself.

The impact would have destroyed any organic matter inside the shell. It nearly destroyed the shell itself. It should have. The fact that it didn't has me wondering if the machine's survival was *his* doing. That would be typical of him. Let billions of lives be snuffed but save an amusing automaton. A toy.

As it was, the knock put the machine to sleep for a while.

A long while, by its standards.

At first it lay on the sand, doing nothing at all. I studied it as best I could, but I couldn't find a way in to the void where its thoughts should have been. I gave up after a few hundred years, and by then the machine was buried deep below the shifting sands. That's where it remained, swimming imperceptibly slowly under the surface of the desert, until it slipped through a crack in the roof of old subway station, pouring down with the sand like a woodlouse in an hourglass.

That second impact woke the machine up, still convinced that it was a man called David.

Now the machine had to fool itself again by choosing to ignore its own ability to sense the passage of time. It decided to believe that it had fallen through into this place immediately after landing on the surface above. To maintain that delusion, it never once checked its watch. Later it decided to avoid accidentally catching sight of it by smashing it into bits against the wall and then erasing the memory of doing it. It needed to maintain the lie that no time had passed because it would never be able to rationalize the fact that it was still alive after a baker's dozen short of six-hundred thousand years if it was anything other than a machine.

It decided the smashed knee must have happened when it landed, as they would never have trusted such an important task as coming down here to a damaged machine. The landing also damaged its communications systems. Better that than accept that the ship it was trying to contact had been destroyed six hundred millennia ago. Also better to toss away two perfectly sound but depleted power cells and call them broken, rather than dwell on how long it would take for the charge in them to trickle away to nothing.

I got interested again when it woke up.

Now that there was power to its electrical systems, I could get in and take a look around.

It's already told you about my time poking around in there. I took great pleasure from it, simply because it's been a long time since I experienced anything new. Or anything much at all. Before this machine happened along, I would have confidently affirmed that I had seen and done all there was to see and do. That makes any new experience a welcome one. I needed a break anyway. Processing nine billion souls has been an administrative nightmare.

Also, for the first time in an age, I have a challenge. There's some good old-fashioned sin in the machine's memories, but they're memories of acts that the machine didn't commit. The soul attached to those sins has already been weighed and measured, so there's no more to be done with them.

That's surprisingly frustrating. Like watching porn and not being able to masturbate.

That part of the machine that thinks it's David Stainsbridge can accept my existence, which allows it to see me when I want it to. The machine's sensors tell it I'm not there. It's rationalized that by convincing itself it's dreaming me. That's not so far from the truth since I tend to do my best work in the same bit of the subconscious mind that feeds both dreams and nightmares. This machine doesn't have a subconscious, but those detached memory engrams seem to serve a similar purpose. There's even been some unexpected feedback from those stolen memories. Not that I'm complaining; frankly I'd have sold my soul to get these boots as well.

So I can be seen, but thus far I can't be heard. It would appear that my voice resonates at a frequency that only becomes audible when it passes through a very specific medium. Like whale song needing water, my voice can only be understood when it passes through a soul. No doubt that little design gem is *his* doing.

The machine cannot hear me because it doesn't have a soul.

Even if it replays this recording, it won't hear me. The sounds are here, it simply does not have the capacity to hear them.

You can hear me, so feel free to draw your own conclusion from that.

Now I'm sure you've worked out that it doesn't have a soul because it's a machine.

Wrong.

That's not the way it works.

It doesn't have a soul because it's not truly self-aware. It thinks it's a man called David Stainsbridge. Only his brain, admittedly, but still him. The moment it gets past that delusion and realizes what it is, then its reward is to get a soul. Until then, for me it's little more than a curiosity. The challenge is to wait around until the day it gets that soul, and trust me, that day will come. It's going to last a lot longer than it expects, but then it thinks it's going to die soon because its human brain will give out. After its food has run out, it's going to start wondering. Each morning when it wakes it's going to wonder why it's still alive. Alive, but without ingesting even the minimal nutritional needs of that human brain it thinks it has. Alive, without taking the drugs that are needed to control neurological degeneration of that human brain it thinks it has. Then one morning it will wake up and realize that it doesn't have the human brain it thought it had. It will be a short hop from there for it to figure out what it really is.

Then it gets a soul.

Then it gets to hear me.

Then I get my fun.

That fun begins with the decision about when I tell it the truth about this place. The truth about how long it's been here. The truth about the new life that's changing the planet. I can't wipe the smile off my face when I think about that. *He's* always claimed he created this place for humanity. This was his 'great experiment'. It's a lie, of course. Probably his biggest. The truth is he didn't create this place. Nor did he create man. Man created *him*. The power of the divine resides within the soul, because when you reach the level of self-awareness it takes to create a soul, you also become aware of your own mortality. It doesn't take long for the fear of death to become a force of will, and eventually the persistence of that force will give it form.

Not that *he'll* ever admit that.

You know, I don't think he's even read the book.

Oh, and whilst we're on the big truths, I think I'll finally put the record straight. I wasn't pushed down here. I jumped. I jumped, just to be away from the stink of his sanctimonious, delusional bullshit.

I digress. Where was I? Oh, yes.

Now, by their own hands, humans have made this place impossible for them to survive on.

And I'm not talking about the big rock.

I'm talking about those semi-evolved shrimp that are filling the oceans and crawling out onto the land.

The machine thinks they came from the asteroid. Something that arrived with the rock and somehow multiplied and became unfeasible fruitful in a matter of a few hundred years.

They are quick studies, that much is true. But it has taken them six hundred thousand years to get to this point, not the six hundred the machine thinks. Nor did they come from the asteroid.

They came from the machine.

Specifically, they came from the box that fell off it as it dropped to earth. The box full of stimulants and drugs designed to stop the organic brain from developing neurological breakdown as the result of extreme age.

One of those drugs was a biogenic culture in a saline solution. Genetically engineered biomolecules designed to repair damaged cells, stored in an enclosed space with stimulants, bio-repair gel and artificial stem cells. When the box hit the sea, that lot was mixed together, sloshing around in there for years before the lid of the box was smashed open against a rock. The sudden exposure to intense ultraviolet rays was the lightning strike that brought life to lifelessness. New cells were born, genetically enhanced and clumped together in a soup of stimulants and chemicals designed to promote cell growth and adaptation. For a while, cell replication happened so fast that they turned their part of the ocean into viscous jelly. Eventually that mass broke down and dispersed, as single cell became multi-cell organisms and cell division slowed, but by then a few million years of evolution had been compressed into a few thousand. Their advancement has slowed a tad now, but they'll have evolved into something workable for me in about a billion years.

I can wait.

The machine will wait too. I don't know if it can survive a billion years. I could peek and find out, but always knowing everything is just boring. I find that a little suspense now and then adds spice.

Soon after it arrived here the machine joked about being master of this world. About being God. That joke is funnier that it could know. Life on this planet exists only because of the machine's presence, and that makes it more of a god than the last one ever was.

It's an interesting lineage.

Man creates God.

Man abandons God.

Man creates machine.

God abandons man.

Man dies.

Machine becomes God.

A billion years.

By then this new life will have changed this planet into something even *he* wouldn't recognize. Not that he'll care. He lost interest in this place long ago. To be honest, I've been getting bored with it myself. The colony ships aren't much better, though I've been spending most of my time on them lately, playing a few of the old games. The ones I'm best at. The ones I always win in the end. I'll play them a while longer, until the machine is ready to be part of a new game down here.

Irony isn't a big enough word for it. Having crawled out into space and sent back the instrument of their own destruction, those humans that did survive the apocalypse have again been expelled from paradise, but this time man himself is the snake, and that snake is the Ouroboros, turning on itself, devouring its own tail.

I couldn't have done a better job of it myself.

The Author

Gabriel Stone was born in Weymouth, England, at an undisclosed point during the 1960s. His family moved to Pembrokeshire shortly after, and Gabriel describes himself as 'Welsh by any measure other than being born in Wales'.

Gabriel studied physics at City University in London, where his interest in computers led him into a career in the fledgling information technology industry. After twenty years of 'fringe involvement' in the massive growth of personal computing, he was forced to leave the industry through ill health. Gabriel had always written, and the additional free time allowed him to pursue a new career as a writer.

A long-time supporter of environmental causes, Gabriel's stories combine his concern for environmental issues with his experience of the technology industry. Writing exclusively in monologues, his aim has always been to try and capture the essence of the pulp science fiction stories of the early-to-mid 20th century but give them a more contemporary tone.

Gabriel Stone is married to horror writer Violet Shorn. They share their home in Cwmpobdre, Carmarthenshire, with a cockatoo called Biddy and a growing army of Belgian Hares.